The Chase

ALSO BY ALEJO CARPENTIER

Music in Cuba

Explosion in a Cathedral
The Harp and the Shadow
The Kingdom of This World
The Lost Steps
Reasons of State
War of Time

ALEJO CARPENTIER

The Chase

Translated by Alfred MacAdam

Introduction by Timothy Brennan

UNIVERSITY OF MINNESOTA PRESS

MINNEAPOLIS

Originally published in Spanish as *El acoso* by Editorial Losada, S.A., in 1956.
First published in the English language by Farrar, Straus & Giroux, LLC.
First University of Minnesota Press edition, 2001
Reprinted by arrangement with Farrar, Straus & Giroux, LLC.

Published by the University of Minnesota Press
111 Third Avenue South, Suite 290
Minneapolis, MN 55401-2520
http://www.upress.umn.edu

Library of Congress Cataloging-in-Publication Data
Carpentier, Alejo, 1904–
    [Acoso. English]
    The chase / Alejo Carpentier ; translated by Alfred MacAdam ; intro-
duction by Timothy Brennan.—1st University of Minnesota Press ed.
        p. cm.
    Includes bibliographical references.
    ISBN 0-8166-3809-8 (pbk. : alk. paper)
        I. MacAdam, Alfred. II. Title

    PQ7389.C263 A6413 2001
    863'.64—dc21

                                              00-069051

Printed in the United States of America on acid-free paper

The University of Minnesota is an equal-opportunity educator and employer.

11 10 09 08 07 06 05 04 03 02 01   10 9 8 7 6 5 4 3 2 1

Introduction
Timothy Brennan

"*The Chase*," recalled Alejo Carpentier, "is among all my novels the one that probably has the fewest readers, even though [Jean-Paul] Sartre considered it my best."[1] Carpentier's estimate of the novel's readership may be incorrect, but his account of Sartre's praise is undoubtedly true. Fragments of the work first appeared in *Les Temps Modernes* in 1954, and the public reception was glorious when the book appeared two years later in France and (simultaneously) in Buenos Aires. Set in the waning days of the dictatorship of Gerardo Machado in Cuba, and based on a real event Carpentier witnessed shortly after his return to Cuba from Paris before World War II, the novel is not unlike Sartre's "The Wall." Both address the cowardice, heroism, and fate of a political fugitive who is captured in the closing lines by pitiless fascist agents working under the chance occurrences of an existential law.

With its layering of narrative voices and its reverberating spheres of discontinuous time, *The Chase* is furiously cinematic. Its opening scenes seem to have been written for film: the mingling bodies of an overdressed audience during the intermission of a musical performance, the architectural grandeur of old Havana, the sweaty rumpled clothing of a frightened young man fleeing from the authorities. If the work looks forward to Alfred Hitchcock's portrayal of a murder in a concert hall in *The Man Who Knew Too Much*, it is only a sign that Carpentier also understood the importance of mise-en-scène in portraying psychological terror.

Several of Carpentier's novels seemed poised to become movies during the 1950s when his fiction reached international audiences for the first time. Tyrone Power actually bought the rights to *The Lost Steps*, raised the money, and went as far as writing the production schedule (Ava Gardner was to play Mouche)—but then Power unexpectedly died.[2] *The Chase* had inspired no less than Luis Buñuel, who, according to Carpentier, promised to bring this tale to the screen, even if the Spanish director had the habit of working slowly: "*The Exterminating Angel*," recounted Carpentier, "which has just come out in Paris, is a film that [Luis] spoke to me about for five or six years before it appeared. Now it's been at least three years since he announced he was turning *The Chase* into a film, but he still hasn't done so."[3] In the end, only Carpentier's *Reasons of State* (*El recurso del método*, 1974) found its way into movie theaters in a joint Cuban, Mexican, and French production directed by Miguel Littín in 1978.

The Chase was to be realized less in images than in sounds. One could call it a work of music transposed into literature, and not just because the action unfolds in an auditorium during the performance of a symphony. Carpentier consciously applied to the novel the methods musicians used to construct the sonata form. "My musical formation," Carpentier explained, "has given me a permanent feeling for structures."[4] He considered that composers had an advantage over authors, because musicians imposed arbitrary formal limitations from the outset, which gave them a paradoxical freedom to hold the various parts of the work in balance "while subordinating them to a stable and central motif." He elaborates his specific strategy in *The Chase*:

> In this case, it was a matter of scholastically applying the sonata form—a form with a narrative and variations. . . . So, I had my theme "C," which is the ticket seller, who is going to have a smallish role during the story because the central motif is going to be divided into a series of chapters in which the recurring "flashback" (as they say in cinema) consists in our seeing the life of the Hunted One before the tragic night in which he is unable to flee death. His death is as absolutely inevitable as fate in a Greek tragedy, which was my point of departure for the novel as a whole. . . . Theme "A" begins with the entrance of the Hunted One, which is a monologue of fear. . . . Theme "B," Estrella, who is going to appear afterward. The central section is simply a number of variations on Theme "A."[5]

The action of the story is meant to unfold in precisely the time it takes to perform Beethoven's *Eroica Symphony*, the symphony performed in the second half of the concert that the Hunted One feverishly attends in the course of the novel. According to his own account, Carpentier calculated the time it would take for someone to trace the itinerary followed by his hapless protagonist through the streets of Havana: "forty-six minutes, exactly."[6]

The novel appeared in the white heat of Carpentier's most productive period of fiction writing during the later 1940s and 1950s when he was busy transforming himself from music critic and radio arranger to novelist. The period was marked by his return to Cuba after more than a decade in Parisian exile working as an avant-garde librettist and radio artist. Having left Cuba for Paris in 1928 (at the age of twenty-four), Carpentier fled the dictatorship of Gerardo Machado at a time when Cuba was under the more or less complete control of the United States. Making his living in Paris as a chronicler for the upwardly mobile back home, he was employed by Cuban newspapers that were most interested in uplifting accounts of the European salon and concert scene. And that is what he produced for them, writing for magazines and journals such as *Chic* and *Carteles*.

Later heralded as the inventor of magical realism and honored by contemporaries Edith Sitwell and Roger Caillois as the greatest novelist of the century, Alejo Carpentier was, in his own mind at least, and for the first part of his career, primarily a music critic. Living a little more than a decade in Paris between the wars, Carpentier spent his years of apprenticeship experimenting with the art of radio and composing enough music reviews to fill over four volumes. He had been brought up on a strict literary diet of Balzac, Zola, and Flaubert. Although born and raised in Cuba, Carpentier had studied in Paris at the Lycée Jeanson de Sailly before he was sixteen, and he spoke Spanish throughout his life with a French accent. He also spent key parts of his youth and early teens on a small ranch on the outskirts of Havana in "El Lucero," purchased by his architect father in 1915; there he lived among the chickens and geese he would later describe in the last chapter of *The Kingdom of This World* (*El reino de este mundo*, 1949).

In 1922, at the age of eighteen, Carpentier launched his column "Obras famosas" (Great works) for the small Havana weekly *La Discusión*. The articles represented a flurry of highbrow treatments of European classics that also considered work ranging from H. G. Wells and Gogol to the little-known early plays of Georges Bataille, the French surrealist and amateur ethnographer. Apart from giving us a map of Carpentier's remarkably broad early interests, the column prefigured his later program on "great figures" for a Havana radio station during World War II, and betrayed his eagerness to popularize art while showing some of the flair for publicity he would display at Radio Luxembourg and Poste Parisien between the wars. The early journalism also demonstrates that Carpentier, already in 1927, was writing on the "possibilities of AfroCuban music" for the small Havana journal *Musicalia*.

Journalist and reviewer, Carpentier cut his life down the middle. He had returned from the Lycée, in his own words, "an acceptable pianist" and clearly had more designs as a librettist than a novelist in early life: "At the age of seven, I was playing the Preludes of Chopin. And I knew Debussy perfectly . . . I soon succeeded at becoming a tremendous improviser [*repentista*] (I think the word has disappeared from the dictionaries): that is to say, I used to play everything anyone put in front of me."[7] His father, a French émigré and a distinguished cellist, had studied with Pablo Casals; his grandmother had been a protegé of César Franck. His own noteworthy musical career began with the study of composition while attending a secondary school in Havana, where he displayed modernist sympathies from the start. Speaking of a slightly later period, he remarked: "I passed without any difficulty to Stravinsky and Schoenberg and, for that reason (we're talking about 1924), to the discovery of jazz and the return to Bach. Whoever lived during that time knows what I'm talking about."

By 1936, he had had his fill of Paris, and wished to free himself (as so many of his French contemporaries did) from the grip of surrealism in order to find different solidarities. He came back to his native capital on the eve of World War II. During a prodigious stint in Havana between 1939 and 1945, he made himself into one of the most recognizable radio personalities in all of Cuba. He sponsored the first exhibition of Picasso's paintings in Havana (and in Latin America), introduced Cuban audiences to the new music of the atonalists, and wrote librettos for Cuban composers such as Amadeo Roldán and Alejandro García Caturla. Above all, he researched and wrote his first true masterpiece, *Music in Cuba* (*La música en Cuba*, 1946), a book that not only would become the model for all writing on black underground music cultures and "salsa" decades later but that also taught Carpentier the history of Latin America, giving him a taste for the archive on which he would later rely when writing fiction. He would proclaim, "*Music in Cuba* prepared me to write all the later novels."[8]

In 1945 he left Cuba for Caracas, Venezuela, where he flourished as director of the radio station Publicidad Ars and founded the column "Letra y solfa" (Letter and [musical] note) for the newspaper *El Nacional*. While he was living on a *finca* outside Caracas between 1945 and 1959, Carpentier's most productive fiction writing took place. Also, from this region in the South American mainland he traveled in 1947 to the vast wild interior of the Gran Sabana, describing the trip later in his "Visión de América," a collection of five articles for the Cuban magazine *Carteles*. This attempt to understand the cultural significance of "la selva" (the forest or jungle) for the Latin American historical self drove him the following year to undertake an expedition to the upper Orinoco in Guyana, traveling through Ciudad Bolívar, then embarking to Puerto Ayacucho and on to San Fernando de Atabapo in the heart of the terrain occupied by the Guahibo Indians in some of the least-known regions of Venezuela. The trip would form the basis for *The Lost Steps* (*Los pasos perdidos*, 1953).

The Chase, then, belongs to a constellation of work that marked a severe career departure for Carpentier, who was in his midforties before he had composed any of the novels for which he is famous today. Within that constellation, *The Chase* is at once typical and exceptional. If assembling the documents for *Music in Cuba* had given him the historical repertoire for his later fiction, that fiction itself was structurally, and anecdotally, musical. Carpentier's novels would eventually change the international scope of Latin American fiction by being the first to articulate the peculiar array of styles and themes later used to such wide effect by the "boom" novelists (including Gabriel García Márquez, Mario Vargas Llosa, and Carlos Fuentes). He provided North American and European readers with portraits of a *political* (rather than merely racial) other.

If Carpentier managed to transform an exoticized

homo tropicalis into a political agent in a history that actually happened (the Haitian revolution, the French takeover of colonial Guadeloupe, the Spanish Civil War, and so on), he also helped overcome a standard U.S. prejudice against dramatizing politics itself, something that tended to make Caribbean fiction, in American eyes, all the more foreign. *Music in Cuba* was always a political affair, and the thrill of making new connections in the music project—as well as a good deal of the material that project unearthed—found its way into the series of novels known as the "American cycle." Indeed, music is integral to all of Carpentier's novels, beginning with the musician antihero of *The Lost Steps*, who sets off on a journey to the upper Orinoco to discover the origins of primitive music. In *The Baroque Concert* (*El concierto barroco*, 1974), one finds an imaginary convocation of Handel, Scarlatti, and Vivaldi; again in *The Harp and the Shadow* (*El arpo y la sombra*, 1979), there is a depiction of the dangerous sensuality that was imported to Spain with Caribbean rhythms. Even his Marxist novel-memoir of interwar Europe—the great, late work he wrote while serving in Castro's government, *La consagración de la primavera* (The rite of spring, 1978)—begins by invoking its namesake, Igor Stravinsky's "Rite of Spring."

The Chase, however, is not one of the American cycle, and so it is anomalous even if written in the exact middle of Carpentier's project to reinvent Latin America as modernity's largest open secret. The novels of the American cycle tended either to be built out of meticulous factual details surrounding key figures in the history of the Americas (Henri Cristophe and Mackandal in *The Kingdom of This World*, and Victor Hugues and Robespierre in *Explosion in a Cathedral* [*El siglo de las luces,* 1962]) or settings and situations designed to teach international readerships about the physical and historical reality of the Americas as a place (Rosario, the Adelantado, and the Cliff of the Petroglyphs in *The Lost Steps*).

Despite not belonging to the factual renditions of the American cycle, *The Chase* is based on an actual event. Shortly after returning to Havana from Paris in 1939, Carpentier attended a production of Aeschylus's *Eumenides* with friends. At the exact moment when Orestes was going to kill Clytemnestra, entering the palace behind whose walls one could hear a terrible cry—at just that moment a shot rang out somewhere at the back of the audience in the Havana theater, with Carpentier present. He and his friends did not know until the next day what had happened: a gang member had been gunned down right there in public during the performance without anyone recognizing the difference between reality and performance. "I found it very interesting," observed Carpentier, "this irruption of real tragedy in the midst of Greek tragedy."[9] It reminded him of André Malraux's description of the work of Faulkner as "an irruption of Greek tragedy in a police novel."[10] Carpentier wryly pointed out that *The Chase* was, in that sense, an exact inversion of Faulkner: a police novel irrupting in a Greek tragedy.

As if it were an antique backdrop, the sites and smells of Havana make the novel an internal, inwardly directed work whose echoes can be found in the opening chapter of *Explosion in a Cathedral*, which depicts the filthy opulence of late eighteenth-century Havana, and equally in Carpentier's photo-essay on the city's baroque architectural wonders, *La ciudad de las columnas* (City of

xiii

columns, 1970). His extravagant vocabulary is often architectural, and he speaks of "bucraniums," "astragals," and "fleurons." That purposive diction suggests something of the confusion surrounding the word "chase," which does not capture Carpentier's title in Spanish: *el acoso* means a harrying, relentless pursuit, redolent of the Furies themselves.

Carpentier's political profile is central to the novel. Like *Explosion in a Cathedral*, the book anatomizes revolution, and like *The Lost Steps*, it explores the paradox of the intellectual and the aesthete against the backdrop of more plebeian necessities. The novel's world is that of student revolutionaries fighting a dictatorship that for the moment has the upper hand—the very world that Carpentier left for Paris and, to his disappointment, found again on his return. Not every revolutionary is adequate to the tasks demanded by revolution: "*The Chase* is perhaps my only novel that can be said to appear pessimistic, even a little desperate, because it is the story of an utterly useless project."[11] The protagonist's failure of nerve, his collapse into Christian mysticism, and his eventual betrayal of his comrades all make him an unheroic counterpoint to Beethoven's *Eroica*. A North American is likely to see these ironies as a fable of the follies of rebellion, but that would be to miss Carpentier's meaning. The tragedy is that the Hunted One rebelled for the hell of it, forgot his original motives, and died before the victory.

Notes

1. Virgilio López Lemus, ed., *Entrevistas: Alejo Carpentier* (Havana: Editorial Letras Cubanas, 1985), 274. This quotation is from an interview with *La Quinzaine Littéraire* in Paris, July 1975.

2. *Entrevistas*, 45, 47. Interview with *Sociales* in Havana, May 1957.

3. *Entrevistas*, 92. Radio interview with *Radio-Televisión Francesa* in Paris, 1963.

4. *Entrevistas*, 48-49. Interview with *Nuestro Tiempo* in Havana, March-April 1958.

5. *Entrevistas*, 384-85. From *Afirmación literaria americanista*, in *Colección Encuentros* (Caracas: Facultad de Humanidades y Educación, Universidad Central de Venezuela, 1978).

6. Ibid., 385.

7. *Entrevistas*, 226. Interview with *Triunfo* in Madrid, June 1974.

8. Araceli García-Carranza, *Bibliografía de Alejo Carpentier* (Havana: Editorial Letras Cubanas, 1984), 19.

9. *Entrevistas*, 382-83. From *Afirmación literaria americanista*.

10. Ibid., 383.

11. *Entrevistas*, 92. Radio interview with *Radio-Televisión Francesa* in Paris, 1963.

The Chase

Sinfonia Eroica, composta per festeggiare il souvvenire di un grand'Uomo, e dedicata a Sua Altezza Serenissima il Principe di Lobkowitz, da Luigi van Beethoven, op. 55, No. III delle Sinfonie . . . The startling crash of the slamming door shattered his childish pride at having understood those words. The fringes of the red curtain swept past his head, ruffling several of the book's pages, then swung back into place. Torn from his reading, he associated ideas of deafness—the Deaf Composer, his useless ear trumpets—with the sensation of once again hearing the din around him. Surprised by the sudden downpour, the people lingering on the grand staircase returned to the lobby, laughing, jostling those standing there, shouting to each other over bare shoulders, all of them confined in the building

3

by the deluge that collected in the hollows of the awning before pouring out in torrents onto the granite steps. Even though the crowd was being called back to their seats a second time, they all lingered there, clustered together, breathing the moist scents of green poplars and watered lawns. It refreshed their sweaty faces, the breath of the earth mixing with the tree bark, whose cracks had begun to close after the long drought. The suffocating evening having passed, their bodies relaxed, a relief they shared with the plants that had opened among the pergolas in the park. The flower beds, edged with boxwood, gave off the vapors of freshly plowed fields. "This is good weather for you-know-what," someone whispered, looking at the woman leaning against the bars of the box office, her profile hidden by her fox stole. She seemed unconcerned that the ticket seller behind her was a man, as she had just disengaged herself from the confinement of a most intimate garment—evidently not caring that he saw her do it—in one matter-of-fact, nonchalant movement. "In a cage like a monkey," said the ushers, mocking this ticket seller who was so different from the other ticket sellers, remaining, as he would, until the end of the concerts even though he was free to leave at ten, after locking up the money and the tickets—the Regulations stated: "Half an hour before the end of the performance." He wanted to humiliate the woman in the fox stole by making her understand that he had seen her, so, with a cashier's trick, he slid a handful of coins over the narrow marble slab in front of him. The woman, now visible in profile, stared at his hands floating over the coins—no one ever looked at anything but his hands—and repeated her gesture.

Such immodesty was proof he did not exist for the women who filled the lobby, trying to stand where a mirror would reflect their coiffures and gowns. The furs they wore in spite of the heat made moisture collect on their necks and bosoms. To relieve themselves of the weight, they would let their stoles slip down, draping them from elbow to elbow across their backs as if they were thick festoons in a painted hunting scene. His eyes fled from what was so near yet so unattainable. Beyond the flesh lay the park with its columns abandoned to the cloudburst, and, beyond the park, behind the doorway in shadows, the mansion with the Belvedere—once upon a time a manor house surrounded by pines and cypresses, now flanked by the ugly modern building where the ticket seller lived, just under the last chimneys, in the maids' room, whose skylight looked like yet another geometric figure among the abstract design of rhombuses, circles, and triangles. Next door, in the mansion, whose old structure was crumbling above urns and balustrades, but which at least retained the prestige of a style, a wake must have been in progress, since the terrace, always deserted because it was either too sunny or too dark, had been swarming with shadows until the first thunderclap burst. From his vantage point in the ticket booth, he tenderly contemplated that broken-down apartment, now fallen into the careless hands of the poor, which looked so much like the badly lighted dwellings in his hometown. There, when a death occurred, the lighting of the candles amid crumbling walls, bird cages draped with tablecloths, furniture whose poverty was magnified by the presence of the glittering silver of the candelabra, caused the rooms to take on something of the sumptuous illumination of a tabernacle. Having a wake meant pomp under the tile roof and its rain gutters, the presence of silver and bronze, the solemnity of dignitaries in mourning clothes, and bright lights that sometimes revealed too much—the cobwebs woven between beams or the dark sawdust left by woodworms. (Then, those who like him were studying some instrument had to explain to the neighborhood that practicing did not mean breaking the mourning period and that studying "classical music" was compatible with the grief one felt for the death of a relative.) *In those days he hid his infirmity from everyone; he lived alone with his demons: wounded love, hope, and pain.* If he was there, perched on the stool, leaning against the worn damask curtain, in that ticket booth as narrow as a desk drawer, it was so he could learn to understand great things, because he admired things others kept behind closed doors, locked away from his poverty. That awareness revived his pride as he stared at that soft back, which looked as though it were being pressed by a thumb at each shoulder blade. Her stole hanging low, she was leaning against the thin bars, so near to his hand. *"The courage I possessed so often in the days of summer has disappeared," he writes in his Testament. And it is the cold of the grave and the odor of Nothingness. In the lost house in Heiligenstadt, in those days without light, Beethoven screams his death howl* . . . He had gone back to his book, no longer thinking about those who glittered in their jewels and starched shirts, flitting from the mirrors to the columns, from the stairway to the lyres and sistrums held by the sculpted figures in the relief, during that intermission prolonged excessively by the Maestro, who was still making the horns rehearse the trio in the Scherzo, trying out hunting sonatas backstage, behind the curtain. "In a cage like a monkey." But he, at least, knew how the Deaf Genius one day, after smashing the bust of a potentate, had shouted in his face, *"Prince: You are what you are by the accident of birth; but what I am I am because of myself!"* If he took this kind of job at night it was so he could reach a place these bejeweled, decorated figures would never reach, these people who never saw anything but his hands moving over the marble slab. Suddenly the woman moved away from the bars, slipping her stole back up on her shoulders. Shouting out parting words, everyone now hurried back to the hall, whose lights had begun to dim. The musicians were taking their places, picking up the instruments they'd left on chairs; the trombonists went to their seats in the rear; the bassoon players raised their instruments in the middle of all the tuning, itself dominated by a sharp trill; the oboists, after making gluttonous faces as they tested their reeds, lingered over pastoral pauses. The doors closed, except the one that would be left ajar—until the conductor's first gesture—to permit latecomers to enter on tiptoe. At that very moment, an ambulance passed in front of the building at top speed, swerved, and brutally slammed on its brakes. "A seat," said an urgent voice. "Any seat," the man added impatiently, while his fingers slid a bill through the bars of the ticket booth. The ticket books had been put away and, as the ticket taker was searching for the keys to get them out, the man disappeared into the darkness of the theater. Then two more men came

7

up to the booth. And since the last door was closing, they ran in, melting into the other members of the audience, who were already in the hall looking for their seats. "Hey!" shouted the ticket taker. "Hey!" But his voice was drowned out by the noise of applause. In front of him there was a new bank note, tossed there by the impatient man. He must have been a great music lover, but he did not look like a foreigner even though he paid five times the value of the most expensive box to hear a symphony performed at the end of a concert. But his clothes were very wrinkled— like those of people who think, an intellectual, a composer perhaps. *But the man who is dying hears, suddenly, an answer to his prayer. From the depth of the forests that surround him, where he sleeps, under the October rain, he hears the future Pastoral Symphony, he hears the sound of the trumpets in the Eroica, he answers the call of the Testament . . .* The bank note, with its blotting-paper consistency, thick and warm, seemed to swell in his pulsating hand; it became a bridge, parting the bars, piercing walls, stretching toward the woman who was waiting—he could not imagine her in any way except *waiting*—in the half-light of her dining room decorated with plates, making that lazy gesture, one so characteristically hers, as she moved the fan that breathed sandalwood from each of its ribs from her temple to her breasts, from the back of her knee to the back of her neck—finally letting it rest on her lap. The woman he saw during the intermission aroused him with her movements, with the dark fur on her sweaty skin, and with her shoulders warily sharing the coolness of the metal

8

bars. However, the hurried spectator might still return to demand the change from the bill he'd tossed onto the marble with the largess of a great gentleman—besides, the Biography, whose pages were spread open before him, had shown him that Great Gentlemen were not to be trusted. He parted the damask curtain that separated him from the hall, where silence had now frozen the musicians with their instruments poised, with a gesture of resignation, which should have been a gesture of joy after such a long preparation, after such an anxious wait. *Sinfonia Eroica, composta per festeggiare il souvvenire di un grand'Uomo.* Two dry chords resounded, and the cellos sang a hunting-horn theme, under the quivering tremolos. *This opening exists in three states in the notes collected by Nottebohem,* said the book. But the book was slammed shut. The reader breathed in the smell of earth, leaves, and humus that entered the empty lobby, reminding him of the back yards of his hometown after a rain, when the staves of the washtubs were strained to their limits and the ducks joyfully splashed around in the muddy water. That was the same smell that came—after summer thunderstorms—from the toolshed, where, perched on a broken incubator, looking through a hole where a brick had fallen out, he had so often contemplated the Widow taking a bath; hardened by her perpetual mourning, her body was still so smooth under lather that lingered on her belly and then ran slowly, foaming, down her thighs, toward legs that suddenly became those of an old lady below the knees. He had learned the secret of that smooth bosom, that arched

9

waist, all, as it were, expressly made for a man's arms, to the tune of a nagging, acid voice, tired of giving lessons to the neighborhood children, and ankles worn out from walking the same routes. Now, the memory of the person who had, not long before, taught him music, even as he, keeping the beat, carefully sought out what was hidden under garments dyed and redyed black. This, added to the night's incitements, finally overwhelmed his scruples. No one here could boast of having approached the symphony with greater devotion than he, after weeks of study, score in hand, standing before the old records that still sounded fine. The newly famous conductor could not direct it better than the illustrious expert on his records—a man who had met, when he was a student and she a nonagenarian, a woman who had sung in the chorus at the first performance of the Ninth. He could proudly claim the privilege of not listening to what was being played in that concert without being disrespectful to the memory of the Genius. "Letter E," he said, when he noticed that a tenuous phrase played by flutes and the first violins had begun. And he ran down the stairs, spattered by a rain that bounced off the heavy ironwork of the streetlights. Even the woolly smell of his wet clothing seemed delightful, intimate, and complicitous, because suddenly he felt himself to be the possessor of that bank note which would make him the owner of the house without clocks—whose doors would stay locked even if visitors knocked and shouted—for an entire night. And after waking up together, hearing the squabble of the canaries, there would be one last tussle in the kitchen; the fire burning under the breakfast pots with the fan smelling of sandalwood, and the taste of the crackers slid at dawn into the mailbox—where the sun that beat down on the house across the street, passing over the feathered headdress of the Indian Girl on the bakery sign, kept them hot.

(. . . this pounding that elbows its way right through me; this bubbling stomach; this heart above that stops beating, piercing me with a cold needle; muffled punches that seem to well up from my very core and smash on my temples, my arms, my thighs; I breathe in gasps; my mouth can't do it; my nose can't do it; the air only comes in tiny sips, fills me, stays inside me, suffocates me, only to depart in dry mouthfuls, leaving me wrenched, doubled over, empty; and then my bones straighten, grind, shudder; I stand above myself, as if hung from myself, until my heart, in a frozen surge, lets go of my ribs so it can strike me from the front, below my chest; I have no control over this dry sobbing; then breathe, concentrating on it; first, breathe in the air that remains; then breathe out;

now breathe in, more slowly: one, two, one, two, one, two . . . The hammering comes back; I am shaking from side to side; now sliding down, through all my veins; I am smashing at the thing holding me in place; the floor is shaking with me; the back of the chair is shaking; the seat is shaking, giving a dull push with each shudder; the entire row must feel the tremor; soon the woman next to me will look at me; picking up her fox stole; the man next to her will look at me; they will all look at me; again my chest freezes; I have to breathe out this locked-in mouthful of air that swells my cheeks. Having felt my breath on the back of his neck, the man sitting in front of me turns around; he looks at me; he looks at the sweat dripping from my hair; I've attracted their attention; they will all look at me; there is a clamor on the stage, and they all look toward the clamor. I must not look at that neck: it's scarred by acne; it would be there, exactly there—the only place in the hall—so that the very thing I should not look at is near me. It might be a Sign; my eyes will try to avoid it, looking above it, below it, finally making me dizzy; I must clench my teeth, clench my fists, calm my stomach—calm my stomach—I must stop that running sensation in my guts, that breakdown of my kidneys which sends sweat to my chest; one thrust and another, one jolt and another; I must tighten myself up, cover up the falling apart inside, cover up what's flowing out of me, boiling out of me, piercing me; I must tighten myself up over the thing that's drilling, and burning, in this immobility to which I am condemned, here, where my head must remain at the same height as every other head. I believe in God the Father Almighty,

Maker of Heaven and Earth, and in Jesus Christ, His only Son, Our Lord, who was conceived by the Holy Spirit, born of the Virgin Mary; suffered under Pontius Pilate; was crucified, died, and was buried; He descended into Hell; the third day He rose again from the dead . . . I can't fight much longer; I'm trembling from heat and cold; clasping onto my wrists, I can feel them shake the way a chicken whose neck has just been broken shakes when it's thrown onto the kitchen floor; I must cross my legs, worse yet; it's as if my upper thighs were flowing into my stomach; everything's falling, spinning, boiling in foam that flows all over me, that falls off my sides, that crosses over me, from hip to hip; a bubbling that the others will hear if they turn when the orchestra plays more quietly; I believe in God the Father Almighty, Maker of Heaven and Earth; I believe, I believe, I believe. Something suddenly calms down. "I feel better; I feel better; I feel better"; they say that by repeating something over and over you can make yourself believe . . . What was boiling seems to have quieted down, settled, stopped somewhere; it must be the effect of the position I'm in; I must hold it this way, not move, keep my arms crossed. The woman gestures impatiently, holding her fox stole in front of her; her evening bag slips and falls; everyone turns; she doesn't bend over to pick it up; they think I'm the one who made the noise; the people in front look at me; the people behind look at me; they must see that my skin is yellowed, that my cheeks are sunken. My beard has grown in these last hours; it bristles against the palms of my hands; I look odd to them, with my shoulders soaked with the sweat

14

that's dripping slowly off my hair again, flowing down my cheeks, down my nose. Besides, my clothing doesn't fit in with all this finery: "Get out of here," they'll say to me. "He's sick, he smells." There is another burst of sound on the stage; everyone turns to pay attention to the burst of sound . . . I have to maintain my immobility; put all my energy into not moving, into not calling attention to myself, into not calling attention to myself, for God's sake. I'm surrounded by people, protected by their bodies, hidden among their bodies; my body mixed in with many bodies; I've got to stay surrounded by their bodies; later, I'll leave with them, slowly, through the door where there are the most people, the program right up to my nose, reading it as if I were nearsighted; better still, if there are lots of women, to be surrounded, encircled, encompassed . . . Oh! those instruments beating against my guts, just when I was feeling better; that man pounding those kettle drums, pounding me, each time, right in the center of my chest; those up higher, who are playing so loud right toward me, with those sounds that come out of black holes; those violinists seeming to saw the strings, tearing, grating on my nerves; all this grows and grows, hurting me; two drumbeats; one more and I'd shout; but it's all over; now we have to applaud . . . They all turn around, look at me, hush me up, each with his index finger raised to his lips; I'm the only one who clapped; only me; all around me people are looking at me; from the balconies, from the boxes; the entire theater seems to turn toward me. "Stupid!" The woman with the fox stole also says, "Stupid, stupid,

15

stupid"; they're all talking about me; they're all pointing at me; I feel those fingers stuck into the back of
my neck, into my back; I didn't know it was forbidden
to applaud here; they'll call the usher: "Get him out
of here; he's sick, he stinks; look how he's sweating"
. . . The orchestra starts to play again; something se-
rious, sad, slow. And it's the strange, surprising,
inexplicable sensation of knowing *that*, what they're
playing. I don't understand how I can know it; I've
never listened to one of these orchestras, and I don't
know anything about the music people listen to like
this—like that man over there with his eyes closed;
like those people over there, sitting with their hands
clasped—as if they were involved in something sacred; but I could almost hum the melody that's beginning now, and keep the beat in that stop-and-put-
one-foot-forward-and-then-the-other rhythm, slowly,
as if walking, and enter into something where that
acid-sounding song dominates; and then the flute, and
then those drumbeats, so strong, as if everything had
stopped just so that it could start up again. "How
beautiful this funeral march is!" says the woman with
the stole to the man on the other side. I know nothing
about funeral marches; a funeral march can't be beautiful or agreeable; perhaps I heard one, back there,
near the tailor shop, when they buried the black veteran and the band escorted the gun carriage, with the
drum major walking backward: And they get dressed
up, they put on their frills, even get out their jewels
to come to listen to funeral marches? . . . But now I
do remember; yes, I remember; I remember. For days
and days I listened to this funeral march without

16

knowing it was a funeral march; for days and days I had it next door to me, enveloping me, echoing in my sleep, usurping my waking hours, contemplating my terrors; for days and days it flew over me, like the shadow of an evil shadow, moving in the air I breathed, weighing down on my body when I collapsed at the foot of the wall, vomiting the water I'd drunk. It couldn't be just a coincidence; *that* was being played in the house next door because God wanted it that way; human hands did not put it there, so close, that music of a passing funeral procession, of muted drums, of veiled figures; it was God in the *afterwards*, just as the fire is already in the unkindled wood before the fire starts; God, who did not forgive, who did not want my prayers, who turned his back on me when in my mouth were echoing the words I learned in the book with the Cross of Calatrava on it; God, who threw me into the street and made a dog bark in the trash; God, who put so close to my face this horribly scarred neck, the neck that must not be looked at. And now He is incarnate in the instruments He makes me listen to, tonight, conducted by the thunder of His Rage. I appear before the Lord manifest in a song, as He might also be manifest in the burning bush: as I glimpsed Him, dazzled, illuminated, in that burning coal the old lady raised to her face. I know now that a sinner could never be more observed, better placed in the balance of the Divine Gaze, than one who fell into prison, the supreme trap—brought by His inexorable Will to a place where a language without words finally reveals to him the expiatory meaning of these last days. We have all been given roles in this theater, and

17

the outcome has already been established in the *afterwards—hoc erat in votis!*—just as the ash is already in the wood about to kindle . . . Don't look at that neck, don't look at it; fix your eyes on a spot on the floor, on a stain in the carpet, on the tambourine up there decorating the frame around the stage; God the Father, Maker of Heaven, have mercy on me; I haven't invoked you in vain; you know how I thought of you in my pain; I still believe in your Mercy, I still believe in your infinite Mercy; I've been too far away from you, but I know that often only a second of repentance—the second it takes to call your name— has been enough to deserve a gesture of your hand, the relief from torment, from the confusion of packs of dogs . . . The funeral march is over, suddenly, the way a person, after hearing a plea or being implored, answers with a simple "Yes!" that makes other words useless. And that was when I said I believed in His Mercy. Silence. Time of relief, of rest. The conductor prolongs that silence, with his head bent forward, his arms at his sides, so that something remains of the part that's finished. My veins are not pounding so much, and my breathing isn't painful. This time it doesn't occur to me to clap . . . "Let's see how the . . . [what?] . . . sounds," says the woman with the fox stole, not even looking at the program. A word I couldn't make out. I understand now why the people in my row don't look at their programs; I understand why they don't applaud between sections: the parts have to be played in their own order, the way in Mass the Gospel comes before the Credo, and the Credo before the Offertory; now comes something like a dance; then the hopping, happy music, with a finale of long trumpets like the ones the angels play on the organ in the cathedral where I made my First Communion; there must be fifteen, maybe twenty minutes left; then everyone will applaud and the lights will go on. All the lights.)

The house was still warm from a very recent presence that lingered in the disorder of the bed, which was surrounded by the yellow butts of hand-rolled cigarettes. "Wait," she said, going to change the sheet and plump up the pillows. (The canaries, asleep in their cage: smells of feathers, birdseed, and bread crumbs. The sleepy dog, trained not to bark, pokes his nose in. The moisture stain on the wall that looked like a blurry map. The beams above stained dark red, copying the imitation mahogany in small-town parlors. The pail left in the patio so she could wash her hair with rainwater tomorrow. And the presence of the pink soap, the kind with disinfectant in it.) And it was the perfume that he always rediscovered with delight, because his sense of smell automatically linked it with

20

her waiting nakedness. "Conditioned reflex," he said to himself, noting, as always, that from the moment he knocked at the door his thoughts, sensations, and acts followed each other in a fixed order, the same order as last time, the same as next time. "Today" repeated itself in desire without date—it could be the "today" of yesterday or of tomorrow—one that was reborn with identical words in the presence of the decorative plates in the dining room or after saying that the cat with a bell on his collar sleeping in its basket was beautiful. Their conversation always began the same way: He hadn't visited lately because he was very busy with his studies; she hadn't been going out and wasn't in love with anyone else. He had seen a lamp that he promised to bring her on his next visit. (It could also have been a box of nougat candy or an embroidered cushion . . .) She would laugh, not believing him. She would sit on his lap for a few minutes, and then their conversation would die as she got up to turn on the night-table lamp, after covering the statue of the Virgin of Charity with a cloth. But this time things were different: "You almost didn't find me here. A few days ago they threatened me; they were going to run me out of the neighborhood, they were going to send me to the women's prison. Me, who never makes any trouble." He stroked her with anxious hands, caressing the warmth in the crook of her knee. "I'm staying the night," he whispered in her ear, eager for her to lock up the house. But he found her strangely inert, upset, obsessed with her idea. "I'm not going to any women's prison; I don't want to leave this neighborhood; people around here know I never make trouble." She attached an angry importance to

21

what had happened. Impatiently trying to draw her out of her monologue, he minimized the importance of the event by disdainfully shrugging his shoulders whenever she mentioned those who had threatened her. "It's an Inquisition, an Inquisition—that's what they're up to." She talked in circles, returning to the women's prison, having to leave the neighborhood, the Inquisition, as if she were incapable of thinking about anything else. With each repetition the threat grew, turning into something like the stations along some infernal route. Now she was talking about herself as if she were the only endangered person in the world, the victim of persecution, martyr to an obscure cause, and in that magnification of suffering there was something like an urge to feel sorry for herself because of all the humiliation she'd suffered. "Now they want to know who you're making a life with." The singularity of that expression suddenly reminded him of the roofs and doorways of his rockbound hometown. Up there, where the dragon trees creaked in the wind, where the membranous leaves, the evil orchids, the plants with knife-sharp leaves and thorns wove themselves together in moist tangles that held the dew from dawn until dawn—there, at night, among the battlement-like cliffs, the wolf-dog bitches, the descendants of bitches who had run away from slave-hunting dogs centuries back, would thrust out their muzzles. And those muzzles, howling above their anxious flesh, in the clamor of heat, would call so loud that the dogs below would raise their heads and whine without daring to step beyond the boundaries of their own back yards. Exasperated by the wait, the females would come down to the edge of town and turn the smell of their desire to the breeze so that the dogs would come to break them, penetrate them—drag them, bitten, stone-bruised—until they fled at dawn to the high caves, where they would give birth. "They come to make a life," the village boys would say when they heard the barking of the thirsty bitches panting on the nearby paths, just beyond the first lights, their teats dragging in the dust: "They come to make a life." "And now," she was saying, "they want to know who you're making a life with." Impatiently, he kissed her without finding that softness, that instinctive molding of her flesh to the hardness of the man. "Now," she went on, "they want to know where the guy who left here went; if he went to the café over in the market to drink his wine with egg yolks." He squeezed her waist, looking toward the newly made bed. "It's an Inquisition," she repeated, emphatically, insisting on the word, which she must have associated with interrogation, jails, chains, and the torture of the innocent, as she confused the Holy Office with some pagan persecution. Perhaps she'd seen the term among the lists of prayers that the rosary and ex-voto sellers displayed in the embrasures of convents or uninhabited houses. There, hung on bars that set them in a jail-like frame, were the Virgins of Sorrows, pierced with daggers; Saint Agatha without breasts; Saint Lucy offering her eyes in a chalice; Saint Rosa of Lima threatened by the Dog with sulphurous breath; and the Anima Sola, with wrists tied together, burned by the flames of her jealousy in an infernal porridge. In these lithographs and garish prints, there were stories of flagellations and strappados, drawing and quarterings, and people eaten alive by beasts,

23

along with Saint Lawrence's grill and Saint Andrew's cross. The woman repeated the word "Inquisition" so often that it must have had a dreadful and mysterious value, which gave greater prestige to the suffering caused by those who had come to threaten her—doubtless the police in search of information about someone who had visited her often. Having thought of herself without a place where she could house her dog, her calico cat, her canaries; having imagined herself on the road to the women's prison, being pointed out on the street that traced what remained of the port, among keels in dry dock, ocean rust, and fortresses made of coal, she must have felt herself to be cleaner, brighter, more at one with her alter ego, who closed the house up to all requests every year during Holy Week, visited the Stations of the Cross, giving large sums to charity and lighting candles at all the altars. "An Inquisition," she repeated, as she absent-mindedly ran her fingers through his hair. "Buy something to drink," he said, tired of her whining, giving her the bank note that was heating his fingers. "And have some biscuits delivered for breakfast," he added, seeing her return with her raincoat on over her slip. "It's no good," she said, handing back the money. "It's no good. The bank notes that have the General with the sleepy eyes on them are no good . . ." "No good?" repeated the man, helpless, examining that paper whose numbers had suddenly lost all power. "No good?" . . . He shrank back into the armchair, as if hoping for mercy, feeling for the few coins weighing down his pockets. That's why the impatient spectator had tossed that money between the bars of the ticket booth with that gesture of largess which, as it turned

24

out, had been a subterfuge. "That's all I have," he said, with his entire voice keyed to hope. "It'll have to be some other time," she murmured, lightly gesturing toward the door, "but tonight I'm really tired." Clutching someone who was returning him to solitude and frustration, he kissed the nape, the arms, and the shoulders of an inert being who now was offering him as much as he might want of her mouth to lead him more docilely to the door. "Don't get wet now," she added. The rain was getting heavier. Angrily running, the man reached the eaves of the market, where the turkeys poked their ragged heads out of their filthy cages. The smell of the farmyard, of chickens, along with whiffs of gardens and plowing, took him back in a flash to the map of the Gran Cañada River, whose bed, bristling with rushes, was the road that had so often allowed him to play the game of Invisible Man. From the back of the house, skirting puddles and quagmires—really invisible—it was possible to go across the entire area; it was possible to learn about deserted kitchens at dusk, along with the first bats flying over pots set to boil; eavesdropping on forbidden dialogues taking place in the shadow of fences; it was possible to hear the creak of the rocking chairs in the sacristy, along with the murmurs of the old ladies gathered to say the rosary, while the Palm Climber would light candles to saints who had nothing to do with the Church, putting lottery tickets underneath the blade of a knife whose handle was a carved rooster's head with a coral crest. Beyond the blacksmith's shed, where the songs that were sung were always filled with rhymed obscenities, there stood a tree trunk, the secret mailbox of a childhood romance: wood where the red ants walked under the envelopes, carrying a larva or a straw. Into that hollow had passed the poems copied out in pencil, the written declarations of love, the lock of hair, and the long candy cane, striped like a barber pole, which he'd bought, averting his eyes from someone who could guess the truth and mock his sincerity. But suddenly the girl had started to grow at such a rate that she seemed to stretch between their dates, ever more hollow-eyed and lankier, turning into a giant among the small children. One day, she refused to hide with him anymore in the hollow near the riverbed, where they would make little flutes out of the pink pine nut seeds, flutes they would pass back and forth to see who could get the better sound. He shrank from the girl who abandoned his world and crouched down so no one in the fields could see her as they walked along the edge of the stagnant water. Her hips filled out, her blouses became tight, and she would no longer allow anyone to sniff her armpits and find out by sticking in their noses that they smelled of sweat, just so they could call her a pig. One afternoon, the wagon that went to the train station brought back a rebuilt piano on whose keyboard the Widow of eternal mourning taught her to play the "Alexandra" waltz by ear. The teas and recitals began then, as well as the women's promenades along the main street, walking with arms around each other's waist, exchanging confidences. It was then that he, in despair, started wanting to learn some showy instrument so he could join the county band, at whose concerts the cornet of clarinet soloists were applauded, their names emblazoned on music stands for greater notoriety . . . This evocation of lost

26

purity brought his irritation against the person who had just thrown him out of her house to its peak. A man might want to believe that a woman like that could be a friend, but she was what they all were: first name, whore; last name, garbage. The book was hurting his arm now—the edge of its binding as sharp as a reproach—amid the stench of the wet turkeys, the guinea hens poking their vulturous heads through the holes in the chicken wire. A green plantain, smashed by a heel, was like a flash in the night. *Sinfonia Eroica, composta per festeggiare il souvvenire di un grand'Uomo*. Despair gave way to shame. He would never get anywhere, never free himself from that maids' room, from pressing his handkerchiefs on the mirror to dry, from worn socks tied up at the big toe with a piece of string, as long as the image of a prostitute was all it took to distract him from the True and the Sublime. He opened the book, whose pages turned blue in the flash of a neon sign: *After that prodigious Scherzo, with its whirlwinds and its weapons, comes the Finale, a song of jubiliation and freedom, with its celebrations and dances, its exultant marches and its laughter, and the rich volutes of its variations. And behold, amidst it all, Death reappears* . . . There was still time to hear some of it. He stopped a taxi and reached the hall just when the first chords of the Finale were ringing out behind the red curtain. The doorman, with no one to take care of, was drowsing over the money drawer in the ticket booth, perched on a high stool. "Is there much to go?" he asked, surprised to see the ticket seller return. "About nine minutes," the ticket seller answered, adding, just to show off, "If it's properly directed, the work should not exceed forty-six minutes." Looking up, he once again saw the old palace appear in the rain, decayed and darkened, with its Belvedere, where the people attending the wake had been forced to take refuge again in the room with the candles. He remembered the old lady who lived there: he had seen her through the skylight in his room, standing up on a bed, amusing himself watching how she watered her plants with a child's watering can—two weeks ago, exactly two weeks ago, because it was his birthday, when, with the small money order he'd received from his father, he had bought himself the *Eroica* on well-worn but still fine-sounding records. The vision of the old lady, wearing a white toque, bent over her old pots of rosemary and mint, had touched his heart. Just like the black women in his rocky hometown, when they left their begonias for prayer at the hour of long shadows, while at the same time the hills echoed with the howls of the bitches clamoring to "make life" with the panting, fearful guard dogs down below. Suddenly it occurred to him that it must have been the old lady who had died. But, no, those old black women lived to be a hundred. Some had even gone around still wearing the ankle chains they'd worn aboard slave ships. When he got paid, he'd visit her—even if he didn't know her—and bring her some old-fashioned candy, the kind sold by the guitar-playing confectioner whose doily-covered trays were filled with sugar icing, saints' bones, powder cakes, meringues, and egg-yolk sweets, covered with green, red, and opalescent sprinkles and filled with mint, grenadine, and absinthe syrups. He had to be sure she was alive, that very night, as a rite of purification. Two weeks before, he had bought the

Eroica to prepare himself for hearing the live performance, in a gesture that to him seemed worthy of Bach, who had gone on foot to Lübeck in order to hear Buxtehude. But when the great night came, he abandoned the Sublime Concept for the heat of a whore. He needed to know the old woman in the night was alive. He needed to know it so badly that he would run to the house with the Belvedere as soon as the Finale was over, to make sure she was not the person for whom the wake was being held.

And these things hast thou hid in thine heart: I know that this is with thee.

Job 10:13

The old lady had withdrawn to her narrow iron bed decorated with Palm Sunday fronds and turned her face to the wall with the humble, resigned gesture of a suffering animal. And after the long night, during which the man who had taken refuge there kept watch over her without being able to call the doctor—much less the Doctor who had died so long before, the one she called out for in the darkness when her tearful breathing became words—his real incarnation began. Until then, all he had to do from dawn until dusk was to stay in the second room listening for the warning sounds on the spiral staircase, where the footfalls slowly grew louder, making the thick wood echo. He read the newspapers the old lady borrowed from the dressmaker downstairs; he bought the overripe fruit the vendor sold off cheaply. He could even satisfy his desire for coffee or have liquor sent up. But he had to spend what little money he had carefully—because he could not change the bill folded up inside his belt buckle until he found out about the Arrangement. But now, after the young doctor the niece called had scribbled a hasty prescription—too many stairs for too little pay—they brought almost no food to the sick woman. Food—real food—crunches between your teeth, holds your spoon upright, has to be cut into pieces, pieces you have to chew, that have the consistency and texture a growing, almost intolerable hunger puts into the hungry man's mind, now transformed into a mouth. The niece would appear at any time she pleased with a bottle of milk or a small pot of broth wrapped in newspaper. Which is why he had to take refuge in the Belvedere, locking from the outside the door that led to the terrace. Many of the people who had come up to visit the old lady had tried to open that door to get rid of the smell of sickness in that rectangle of sun-baked tiles. "Not even she knows where she's put the key," the same masculine voice said every time, shaking the door, which he had braced from behind with stakes and boards wedged against the floor. And so two days already went by without his eating a thing, hidden within those four tepid walls from which the paint was peeling, walking from the Westminster clock, which had neither pendulum nor hands, to the trunk with moldy hasps whose lid still boasted the label where, on a certain day, he had written in thick letters using the tip of a shaving brush dipped in India ink: BY EXPRESS. Fearful always that someone would hear the frame of the rickety old bed creak, his pistol within easy reach, he spent his time stretched out on the floor of that broken-down Belvedere in that decayed seignorial house, whose marble, gray and as worn down as a tombstone, retained a remote coolness amid all the feverish brick, enclosed by the low stone walls—too low to create any shade—that delineated the terrace. At least the nights now were not as terrible as the first ones he spent there: those slow, unending nights he whiled away facedown under the open window, keeping himself from falling asleep, waking himself up whenever his eyes closed, because sleep and death were one in his fear. His open eyes registered the reality of a star, of a complete revolution of the lighthouse lamp, and were suddenly disturbed because an insect had begun to buzz behind the door. A wire on the bed frame broke and snapped in his ear because he'd fidgeted too much; the crickets that devoted themselves to singing inside the trunk, the land breeze that swirled up the soot that had fallen in the corners of the terrace—everything that sounded quiet, or strange, or surprising during those nights served as a repeated expiation for his torture. Nevertheless, just before dawn, when the lighthouse lamp seemed to tire of winking in circles, something like a Pardon descended from on high. He relaxed his guard himself and lowered his eyelids as the sea became pale in the first light, yielding himself to a possibility that never lost its terror but which seemed strangely alien, even desirable to him, as long as he did not awaken once the fear of physical suffering had passed. Because physical pain was unacceptable to him. So unacceptable that, because he could not tolerate pain—not just the stab of a real pain but the

35

merest suggestion of pain—he found himself in this abominable present, waiting for the results of the Arrangement. From those first nights he'd retained the habit of dropping off to sleep at dawn, since during the day he had to stay inside the Belvedere to avoid being seen from the high terrace—a rendezvous for laundresses, a playground for children (the children were to be feared most)—of the modern building that flanked the colonial house which had become a tenement. The modern building had a wide, windowless wall covered by meaningless figures in red, green, and black that reminded him of the disks and signs at a rail crossing—although there, at the University, some studious types, disdained by his group, might have asserted that these heroic-sized hieroglyphics corresponded to a new concept of decoration. At nightfall, after the old lady had said her rosary with the seamstress from downstairs, saying good night with exaggerated yawns so everyone would know she was going to bed, he would slip toward the door, remove the stakes, and, crossing into the second room, take whatever the old woman could offer him in the way of stew or nice, thick pot roast, and the morning newspaper, where he would look avidly for some news related to his own destiny. Often all that would be left of the most interesting page would be the mere outline of shoulder pads or sleeves cut out of the paper for patterns to be used by the students of the Academy of Style—which is what the seamstress called the room with the mannequins and red velvet pincushions bristling with pins where she gave lessons on how to sew simple blouses and skirts. But the fragments that remained and supplied information about those living on the outside still kept him absorbed, rereading apparently insignificant news items—those, for instance, that told about people about to take trips—until the time when the old lady was asleep, the movie marquees were dark, the streets empty, and the persistent cry of a child proved how deeply those around his cradle were sleeping. Then, above the spotlights that left him in shadows, he could walk the length of the terrace, looking at the patios with their areca palms and colorless flowers, where, under the archway of an old coach house, there would suddenly appear in the flash of a struck match a woman fanning her bosom or an old asthmatic man enveloped in the smoke from some burned medicinal paper. Beyond was the back of the saddlery, where the dusty remains of a phaeton with lanterns, on whose oilcloth surface were some half-tanned hides, set out there to dry like trophies from a slaughterhouse. Further on arose the inky stench of a small shop that printed business cards. A bit closer, the stink of the kitchens of the poor, their pots abandoned for today in greasy water, and, on the other side, the lazy bustle of a rich family's kitchen, where two maids were dropping dry knives on the table in time to songs they hummed interminably, songs they barely knew but which they continuously started over and would never finish. Hiding behind the body of the Belvedere from the always frightening terrace of the modern building, he would peek out into the street for a moment, contemplating a world of houses where the Californian, the Gothic or Moorish, dwarf Parthenons, Greek temples with lights and

37

venetian blinds mixed with Renaissance villas whose planks were held up by sick columns among malanga vines and bougainvillea. These were colonnaded streets, avenues, galleries, roads of columns, as bright as day; so numerous were the columns that no city had such a stock, with a disorder of orders that mismatched Doric at the axes of a façade with the volutes and acanthus leaves of solemn Corinthians, pompously erected half a block down, between the clotheslines of a laundry whose broken-nosed caryatids supported wooden architraves. There were capitals covered with pustules burst by the sun, shafts whose fluting was swollen with the abscesses left by the oil paint that covered them. Below there abounded utterly vulgar motifs—rosettes on railings, the dentils that should have been up on the cornices were within easy reach of an outstretched hand—while the cornices themselves supported the socles or pedestals that properly belonged at the foot of the wall; between the telephone wires, like afterthoughts, lay Roman vases and cinerary urns which had acquired a felt-like texture and looked like birds' nests. There were metopes in the balconies and friezes that ran from an ogive to an embrasure. One frieze ran completely around all four sides of the building, as if it had been sold by the yard: the theme of the Sphinx interrogating Oedipus. As they walked from portal to portal, passersby could witness the death agony of the last classical orders used in modern times. And in places where the portal had been demolished in a fit of modernization, the columns hugged the wall, embedding themselves in it, useless because they had no structure to support, finally dissolving into the cement that had

38

hardened on top of them. Nothing of all that had anything to do with what little the man who had been
given shelter had learned at the University—that University which for him had been stored away in the
trunk with the moldy hasps.

BY EXPRESS. *From: Sancti-Spiritus*. The hand put down the worn-out shaving brush it had used to draw the words so elegantly in India ink. The man in hiding contemplates himself in that decisive moment of his life. He sees himself busily putting things into the old trunk, brought to the island so many years before by his immigrant grandfather. The relatives and friends who gather around him and who will soon—this very morning—accompany him to the train station no longer exist in the present. Their voices reach him from far away; from a yesterday he is leaving behind. He does not listen to their advice, the better to enjoy the undefinable delight of feeling he is in a future he has already glimpsed—the undefinable delight of detaching himself from the reality around him. At the end of the journey there will be the capital with the Fountain of the Indian Woman Havana, all made of white marble—just as it appeared in the magazine photo tacked to the wall. The caption recalled that, in years gone by, a poet, Heredia—who was not kept from becoming a member of the French Academy merely because he'd been born in a stupid backwater much like this one—had dreamed in the shadow of the statue. At the end of the journey he will see the University, the stadium, the theaters; he will not be held accountable to anyone; he will find freedom and perhaps, quite soon, a lover, since this last item, so difficult to locate in the provinces, is common currency in a place without iron-barred windows, shutters, and busybodies. The idea makes him take special care in folding his brand-new suit, cut for him by his father in the latest style, which he plans to wear for the first time, with matching tie and handkerchief, when he matriculates. Then he will stroll into a café and order a martini. At last he will know how that drink they serve with an olive tastes. Then he will go to the house that belongs to a woman named Estrella, about whom the Scholarship Student told him wonderful tales in a recent letter. And his father is telling him at precisely this instant not to associate with the Scholarship Student, since it seems he is leading a dissipated life and squanders his town-council stipend on good times—"which leave only ashes in your soul." Their voices reach him from far off. They seem even farther away at the train station, among the peasants who shout to each other across the tracks after a trainload of cattle passes by in a thunderburst of mooing. At the last moment his father buys some honeycombs

41

as a gift for the old lady who offered to give him lodging in her house—it seems she has a Belvedere on the terrace, a separate, comfortable room for the student. And now the express pulls in with its steam engine and there is a tumult of farewells . . . And he'd arrived here, very late at night, with the trunk he was now staring at: here at this Belvedere that the woman who was once his wet nurse, who had come to the capital years before with a rich family who owned the ancient mansion now turned into a tenement. From the first moment, he could see from the decidedly maternal tone of the black woman that she would keep his longed-for liberty on a short leash, carefully noting his comings and goings, chiding and annoying him, and, at the very least, keeping him from bringing women to the Belvedere. For that reason, he decided to move away as soon as he began his studies. And now, after having forgotten the old lady for months—was it she who started whining like that a minute ago, or was it the seamstress's son whimpering?—after having deserted this room such a long time ago, he found here the ultimate refuge, the last one available, next to that provincial trunk, left behind when he moved because the things it contained had ceased to interest him.

But today, when he lifted the lid, he rediscovered the abandoned University in the set of compasses his father had given him; in the ruler, drawing pens, and triangles; in the empty bottle of India ink that still smelled of camphor. There was Vignola's *Treatise*, with the five orders, as well as the notebook where as an adolescent he had pasted photographs of the temple at Paestum and Brunelleschi's dome, Wright's

42

Falling Water House, and a view of Uxmal. Insects had devoured his first pencil drawings; and of the capitals and bases he'd copied on tracing paper, there remained only a yellowish lace that disintegrated in his hands. Then came the books on the history of architecture, on solid geometry, and, at the bottom, on top of his diploma, his Party membership card. His fingers weighed that piece of cardboard, the last barrier that might have saved him from abomination. He was told not to waste his time in cell meetings, or in reading Marxist pamphlets, or in praising remote collective farms with photos of smiling tractor drivers and cows graced with phenomenal udders, when the best members of his generation were falling to the bullets of the repressive police. And, one morning, he found himself dragged along in a demonstration that shouted its way down the University stairs. A short distance later came the collision, the mob, the panic, with stones and roof tiles flying over their heads, women trampled, heads bloody, and bullets lodged in flesh. At the sight of the fallen, he concluded that it was true, these were times that demanded immediate action and not the caution and deliberation of a discipline that sought to temper exasperation. When he joined the impatient group, the terrible game began that a few days before had brought him back to the Belvedere, in search of some final protection, bearing the weight of a hunted body he had to hide somewhere. Now, breathing in the scent of termite-eaten papers, of the camphor of dried ink, he found in that trunk something like a symbol, one only he could decipher, of Paradise before the Fall. And when, for a few moments, he attained a lucidity he had never

43

known, he understood how much he owed to the confinement that forced him to talk to himself for hours on end, searching through the detailed examination of those events for some relief from his present misery. To be sure, a road did exist, an infernal passageway. But when he considered the misadventures that had taken place in that passageway, when he confessed that almost everything in it had been abominable, when he swore that he would never repeat the gesture that had made him stare so fixedly at an acne-scarred neck—a neck that obsessed him more than the howling face he saw in the din of that terrible second—he thought he still might be able to live elsewhere and to forget the time when he'd lost the way. Groans: those were the words of the tormented, the guilty, and the repentant as they approached the Holy Table to receive the Body of Christ Crucified and the Blood of the Bloodless Sacrifice. Under the Cross of Calatrava that adorned the child's small catechism that the old lady had given him, it was possible to hear that pathetic groaning, in prayers for confession, in litanies to the Virgin, in the prayers of the Blessed. With sobs, with supplications, the unworthy, the fallen addressed their divine intercessors, ashamed to speak directly to the One who had spent three days in hell. Besides, all the blame was not on his head. It was the fault of the times, of circumstance, of heroic illusions: the effect of the dazzling words with which on a certain afternoon they had welcomed him—a mere provincial boy, ashamed of his suit, badly cut in his father's tailor shop—behind the walls of the building on whose majestically colonnaded façade were stamped in bronze relief, under an illustrious name, the tall Elzevir letters HOC ERAT IN VOTIS . . . Now he was looking toward the Concert Hall, whose capitals with squared volutes seemed to him a caricature of the ones he associated with the initiation he so despised today. There the sentence imposed by that city on the orders that degenerated in the heat and were covered with wounds was confirmed, their astragals transformed into supports for signs announcing a dry cleaner, a barber shop, a soft-drink stand, counters laden with meat pies, ices, and tamarind drinks, where the sizzle of frying hissed in the shadow of the pillars. "I'll write something about this," he used to say, but he never wrote anything, because of that pressing need to accomplish noble tasks. He survived the epic drinking bouts of those months, the excesses to which they, who risked a lot and challenged a lot in order to find the light at the end of the tunnel, thought they were entitled. He did not know where he would be sent now, since the Exalted Personage was going to determine, for his own greater convenience, the most expeditious route. He would never finish the architecture course he had given up at the beginning of the first term. No matter: he would accept the hardest jobs, the worst pay, the sun on his back, oil in his face, the rickety cot, and the bowl, as phases of a necessary expiation. "I believe in God the Father Almighty, Maker of Heaven and Earth, and in Jesus Christ, His only Son, who was conceived by the Holy Spirit, born of the Virgin Mary." All he remembered was the beginning of the Credo. He was going to get the little book with the Cross of Calatrava on it, which he'd left on the straw-filled mattress, when suddenly he noticed that his hunger had passed. He thought about fish, and he

45

imagined them as repugnant things, with that glassy, flat eye which was barely an eye, a tack stuck into the stench of the scales; he thought about meat and found it repellent, unformed, with its dripping blood; he thought about different kinds of fruit and remembered them acid and cold; he thought about bread and it seemed disagreeable to him, the slime and crunch of the crumbs. He did not want to eat. He offered God the emptiness of his stomach as a first step toward purification. He felt light, rewarded, understood. And it seemed that a dazzling sharpness put him into contact with matter, things, the eternal realities that surrounded him. He understood the night, understood the stars, understood the sea which came to him in the reflection of the lighthouse lantern, which gently tortured him each time its rotation shone it into his eyes. But he did not understand in words or images. It was his entire body, his pores—understanding transformed into being—that understood. His person had integrated itself for an instant with the Truth. He threw himself facedown on the clay tiles that still radiated the day's sweltering heat. All this clarity made him weep, there at the foot of the Belvedere in shadows.

On the fourth day, he awoke in the middle of the afternoon with a muddy taste in his mouth. A slow sweat, the drops seeming to swell out of every pore, rolled out of the shadows under his eyes, down the back of his neck, off his forehead, making him feel yellow, emaciated, filthy through and through. Fortunately, he had no mirror to confirm his suspicion, for that would only have made things worse. He sat up on the mattress as if to disburden his temples of an avalanche of gravel. To make things worse, his penis came alive, painfully, enervated by the throbbing in his chest and stomach. He touched himself and then walked over and sat down on the trunk, astonished that his body retained so much energy despite his hunger pangs. Beyond the barricaded door, beyond the dining room,

47

the old lady's niece was speaking confusedly with the seamstress from downstairs. The woman must have gotten better. She'd gone through the same thing before and cured herself with her concoctions and herbs. But this time the illness had gone on for a longer time. So he had to *think* about eating. He would have to invest his newly won lucidity of the past few days— his joy at not eating—into the will to eat. Since he could no longer count on the old lady for food, he had to think about other possibilities. There had to be edible things in a house, in a room, things people do not usually cook. As a boy, he'd often thought about the flavor a grass soup might have, a leaf stew, a crabgrass salad. Herbivorous animals eat plants that man, too, could probably eat. Besides, who hasn't known the pleasure of chewing on a tender stalk of grass? He looked around: wood, clay, soot. In the besieged cities of ancient times, people actually ate bits of softened leather. They gnawed saddle covers, they boiled bridles, belts, the soft thongs of sandals. And in a flooded mine the men had discovered after a few days that the support beams still had soft bark on them . . . He crawled—so his silhouette wouldn't show against the outside walls of the terrace—to where he could see the patio behind the saddler's shop. Someone had taken away the half-cured hides that had been drying for all that time on the carriage. He was astonished at how absurd it was of him to want to contemplate those unreachable skins, as if their remote odor of the flaying or salting room could provide him some relief. Wood, clay, soot. "When the peasants were forcibly gathered in cities by the wicked Captain General of Spain," the old lady had told him, "they swelled up

48

from drinking so much water." He turned on the faucet and, catching the water in his hands, began to drink it avidly in order to fill his stomach. But the water, warmed by the sun that heated the pipes, reached his stomach with the heavy, hollowing coldness of wet soot. He was doubled over by a violent spasm, and falling forward on his fists, he vomited up what he'd drunk until he was seized with a retching that collapsed his stomach and forced him to arch his back like a poisoned dog foaming at the mouth. Exhausted, he threw himself down at the foot of the wall, his body shaken by whiplash convulsions. He was so overwhelmed by the idea of eating that this idea, the only one he could conceive of, became a command of an almost abstract kind. He was no longer thinking, as he had on the first day of his fast, about his favorite dishes, nor did the image, mixed with nostalgia for childhood, appear in his mind of the grand family kitchen smelling of freshly fried fish—with the unctuous greens of peas, rice dyed with saffron, the crackling stiffness of pastries yielding to teeth—that put unreachable flavors in his mouth, ravaged by so much anxious saliva. These foods lost their difference, because he could only think about *food*, any food, all food, as if he had returned to the hunger of a newborn abandoned at the foot of a church steeple howling its misery, seeking its mother in the stone . . . He heard voices. From the spiral staircase, the seamstress downstairs was calling up to the old lady's niece to come try on a dress. He waited impatiently until her high-heeled shoes echoed, ever more faintly, on the wooden stairs, until their voices stopped next to the sewing machine, which had been brought out to

49

the patio to take advantage of the coolness. Taking down the planks and braces, he opened the door that had isolated him from the rest of the house for four days. The old lady, asleep, moaned softly with labored breath, under her Palm Sunday fronds. Next to her, on a chair, there was a bowl of oatmeal. There was only a dessert spoon, so he sank his shaking hand into the mass crisscrossed by melted sugar. And then it was his tongue, anxious, hasty, astonished to be eating stolen food, that cleaned the plate, to the sound of his hog-like grunts in the depths of the china; his tongue quickly moved to the chair's rush seat to lick up what had spilled. His body then raised itself to its knees, and it was his hand again in the box with the Quaker on it, scraping his nails in the raw oatmeal. Later, the door remained closed. Night began to fall. A dredge down in the bay slowly passed opposite the Belvedere: it seemed to float above the sun that stained the walls of the Concert Hall orange. Under the pergolas, a pack of aroused dogs chased a spotted griffon bitch that barked at the onslaught of the males. High up in the modern building, music was playing: the same music he'd heard so often. First nervous, then sad, slow, monotonous. The person lying on the floor, his stomach simultaneously pained and gorged, sleepy, racked by rumbling bowels, drifting from felicity to nausea, sometimes confused those muffled notes with the muffled noise of the visiting-card printing shop. Behind the door, the old lady began to call out to her niece in a cranky voice, which showed she was feeling better. "You cain' eat so much, aunty," shouted the dark woman, who was returning with her new dress, when

50

she saw that there was barely any oatmeal left in the box with the Quaker on it. "You shuddin' eat so much." And since the Soldier was waiting for her in front of the house, she went off, her heels clicking rapidly down the spiral staircase.

The portentous news was God. God, who had been revealed to him by the light of the old lady's cigar the night before she fell ill. Suddenly, her taking the coal from the brazier and raising it to her face—a gesture he'd seen repeated in the kitchens of his childhood— became magnified in his mind and took on over- whelming implications. Her hand, as it raised the light, carried a fire that came from very far away, a fire that existed before the matter it would consume and change—matter that was merely the possibility of fire until a hand set it on fire. But if that present fire was an end in itself, a prior action was necessary to attain it. And that action required another, and others before it, which could only derive from an In- itial Will. There had to be an origin, a point of departure, a capitular of fire which, through countless eras, had illuminated men's faces. And that First Fire could not have set itself ablaze independently . . . He thought he could see in everything a similar succession, an ineluctable process whereby one thing received energy from other things; nevertheless, that sequence of acts could not be infinite. The strings had to end up, perforce, in the hand of a Prime Mover, the initial cause of everything, stock-still in eternity and endowed with Supreme Efficacy. His father's atheism seemed absurd to him now, in the presence of an image that explained so many things; he was wondering to himself why others before him hadn't thought to prove the existence of God by means of that illuminating insight he'd had looking at a glowing coal. It had to be Sunday, because the day before he'd heard the children in the modern building singing, "Died on Sunday and that is the end of Solomon Grundy." As the church bells called people to Mass, he opened the black-and-gold book with the Cross of Calatrava on it, which dispensed unending illuminations to someone who had grown up far away from the catechism, in a Masonic–Darwinian tailor shop. Every page revealed a beauty in the liturgy he'd never known, giving him the exalting impression that he was penetrating a secret, being initiated, sharing the secrets of a fellowship. He had never thought about these things, though he'd seen them many times. The mere altar cloths, for example, could represent the Shroud wherein His Body was wrapped; the alb, the girdle, and the stole told three episodes of the most transcendant Trial witnessed by men. From the purple vestments, which evoked in his mind the columns of

Pilate's house, he would pass to Calvary, where he would stop, absorbed, at the edge of the Chalice; and after contemplating—after understanding—the Chalice, he would marvel at the discovery of that ever-open sepulcher, always open insofar as the most precious substance was concerned, mystical transposition of the greatest drama: darkness that worked the metal to unthinkable depths; shadow wrapped in the blaze of gems and gold; reverse alchemy that out of the splendor created a long night of waiting for a humanity under sentence. Even water, whose liturgical sense he hadn't understood, spoke now from the flank of the Redeemer. He had, from time to time, been in a church, brought there by his devout aunt when his father was in the capital buying fabric for those of his customers who still requested drill and alpaca. He, too, knelt, sat, and stood before the altar with its baroque moldings without ever suspecting that when the celebrant put on the robes of his office he represented nothing less than the Son of God in His Passion. He had observed the service—amused by everything that was not part of the Mass, staring at the beams in the cupola, where there was always a sleeping bat to be seen—without thinking that right before his eyes the Mystery that concerned him most directly was being performed in an action reduced to its symbolic essence. And now that he had been enlightened, he found in the simple movements that accompanied the Doxology, the Gospel, the Offertory, that prodigious sublimation of the elemental which, in architecture, had transformed the hunting trophy into a bucranium, had transformed the ring of twine

54

that binds the sheaf of branches of the primitive saddle into an astragal of pure Pythagorean proportions. To have carried within himself such powers of understanding, to have been able to perceive those truths and to have turned away from them all in order to hear speeches that ended up justifying both the heroic and the abject! Oh! I believe! I believe He suffered under Pontius Pilate, was crucified and buried, that He descended into Hell and that on the third day He rose again from the dead. I believe He ascended into Heaven and sitteth at the right hand of God the Father Almighty. I believe that from thence He shall come to judge the quick and the dead . . . And there is something like the trumpet of the Last Judgment in the music being played again in the modern building, where someone, delighted by the cheap, harsh-sounding gramophone he's just bought, keeps playing the same music over and over again, sometimes even replaying the same passage. What he plays is like a series of different pieces recorded one after the other, which always follow each other in the same order. First it's something very confused that sounds like bugle calls—a military march that never quite turns into a military march. Then comes the sad, slow, monotonous part. After that, there is a very happy dance. But another military march interrupts it, a military march which never really quite turns completely into a military march: something like the bugle calls in that ridiculous documentary about the French aristocrats who heard Mass before the hunt and had their hounds blessed while the huntsmen in livery played instruments that looked like huge copper volutes. And

that part always ended with music in little jumps—
which resembled those toys very small children play
with, the ones in which two parallel sticks are moved
up and down so that two dolls take turns pounding a
peg with mallets. The next section was made up of
broken waltzes that turned into something majestic
and grand, with trumpets and a brass section, just
like the one that played in Sancti-Spiritus near the
tailor shop on concert nights. And then that happy
final uproar, with the hunting horns again . . . The old
lady's niece was descending the spiral staircase. It was
necessary to open the door to see if the old lady was
asleep, and reach the broth which, as usual, was cool-
ing next to the bed. But now, as he took the bowl to
bring it to his mouth, his hands froze in the air. In
the black woman's surprisingly unwrinkled face, her
two eyes were opening, staring at him with glassy
fixity—with distant and inexpressive intensity—at
him, as he put the bowl down between two medicine
bottles without daring to sip its oils slathered over
turbid lentils and the bony feet of some fowl—the kind
hanging from a hook in the poultry market. The
twisted nails of an old rooster were attached to three
toes covered with gray scales—there was something
human in the wrinkles of their skin—and rested on a
slice of barely peeled pumpkin. He vacillated for a
moment, then defied the fixed stare focused too late
on what could not be restrained, and sank his mouth
into that Sunday soup, snorting and gnawing, before
approaching the carton with the Quaker on it. Then,
his lips still powdered with raw oatmeal, he sought
forgiveness and made the gesture of tucking the old

lady in, pulling the blanket up to her neck. When he touched her cheek, a shock of fear paralyzed him, arresting his entire being: that cheek was stiff and hard, and the clenched fist she'd rested on her temple went right back to her temple with all the obstinacy of rigor mortis as he tried to find some pulse in the cold veins of her wrist. A footfall echoed on the spiral staircase. The clicking heel belonged to the niece, who, followed by some other people, was coming up the stairs. She began to scream just as he, after hastily locking the door behind him, reached the Belvedere. The horror of what happened stupefied him; he squatted on the floor, his back against the trunk, all his attention concentrated in his ears: that lame woman was the seamstress; the velvety, asthmatic stride belonged to the janitor; the clatter of shoe taps on each step was the Soldier—who went downstairs again to get the things necessary for a wake and a burial. The patios filled with the sound of questions called from window to window. And soon, in a confused fuss, the men from the Funeral Parlor came with their ice and candles. With the arrival of family members from far-off neighborhoods—Jesús del Monte, Calvario, Santa María del Rosario—who only remembered one another when they found out their numbers had been reduced, the wake began. Occasionally one of them would pound on the locked door, trying to get to the terrace, and the terror of those first days was now reborn within him. The door itself was firmly braced, so they quickly gave up trying to open it. But now the resistance of the wood was reaching its limit. When they took away the coffin tomorrow, the janitor—who was angry because the key had been lost—would call the locksmith. From his secular arm hung the master key. And when the master key turned in the moldy lock and they saw that the blue door did not move on its hinges because it had been blocked from inside, he would have to give himself up. Not to those men, who could do nothing to him and wouldn't even call the police when they learned he belonged to the world of Those to Be Feared. He would have to turn himself over to freedom—to the street, the crowds, the eyes—which was like being called to appear before a judge. Once again he would be questioning every face, afraid to eat two courses sitting at the same table, intolerably obsessed with discovering the coldness of a hospital in the whiteness of every sheet. It would mean having to get out of bed before finishing a good night's sleep, walking in the shadows, fearful of the echo of his own steps; flesh that withdraws and flees the heat of another's flesh because a piece of ripe fruit falls onto the patio—because the wind closes the venetian blinds in the corridor. When no one had wanted anything to do with him; when he was turned away with horror from people's houses, he had remembered the old lady. She could not forget that a long time before she had carried him at her breast, calling him by such tender names that he was moved when he had been told about it. The old lady, seeing him so emaciated, his shirt torn and dirty under the navy-blue suit he'd put on the better to blend in with the shadows, began to shout that she wanted no scandals in her house and that people who start out bad usually end up worse. She had rented him the Belvedere for a pittance when he'd arrived from Sancti-Spiritus; she had given him

advice like a second mother. And he had walked out—
of course—when he saw he wouldn't be allowed to
bring low-life women into a proper religious house-
hold . . . But he seemed so miserable at that moment,
sitting astride a stool, weeping into his dirty-nailed
hands, that he became again for her the same child
who once almost seemed about to suffocate from
whooping cough in her arms. It was his veins, swollen
and green in his temples, and his neck, the spasmodic
shaking of his shoulders, his vinegary breath, the
muted moan that came from within him after his sobs.
Moved, the old lady brought him up to the Belvedere,
deserted all this time, so he could wait there, hidden—
next to the trunk where all that was left of his University life was stored—until the Arrangement was
made. Oh! Mother of God, Mother Most Pure, Mother
Most Chaste, Powerful Virgin, Merciful Virgin, pray
for us; Mystic Rose, Tower of David, Star of the Morning, Health of Sinners, Queen of Martyrs, pray for us
. . . She who calmed my hunger first with the milk of
her breasts; she who made me know the sin of gluttony
with the smooth carnality of her nipples; she who put
on my tongue the savor of a flesh I have sought out
so many times in young torsos of her same race; she
who nourished me with the purest sap of her body,
giving me the warmth of her lap, the sanctuary of her
hands that dandled me with caresses; she who took
me in when all others threw me out, she lies there in
her black box, enclosed within the roughest planks,
diminutive, her face seemingly shrunken over the ice
that drips into a dented tub, because I, who never even
should have thought it—who never should have ad-
mitted it would be possible of me—have devoured her

bedridden food, wolfed down her cereals, gnawed her chicken bones, sucked down her Sunday broth like a greedy hog. Lord, have mercy on us! Christ, have mercy on us! . . . And in the modern building, that music, so sad, so monotonous and sad, seems like a response for the dead.

No one was surprised to see him appear at the wake, since the old lady had worked from time to time in wealthy houses. "They found the key to the terrace," her niece announced with pleasure when she noticed that an unexpected current of air was moving the candle flames. "Please accept my deepest sympathy," someone said, thinking that if a white man was attending a wake for a black, dressed in a dark-blue suit despite the heat, it was because some distant family relationship linked him to the deceased. He looked at himself over the top of the coffin in the mirror above the console table. His face was so emaciated, so free of the fat that had accumulated in it from heavy drinking over the course of those days when he had no work and was trying to forget the work he'd done, that he

61

felt emboldened by the disguise he'd discovered in his own body. He looked at himself and looked again without finding he resembled himself. Nights of torment had put a deep crease in his cheeks, caused his chin to jut out, given an odd fixity to his eyes, which were shadowed by his hair, hair that was too long and which, because it was too long, he combed in an unusual way. He found something so new in his expression that someone crossing his path in a poorly lighted place might—perhaps—doubt it was he. Besides, his dark glasses, which for him had become a kind of professional tool, also helped him. He gave thanks for the pain he'd suffered during his days of confinement and also for the hunger at the outset, holding them up to the One he felt to be more and more present, as if He, too, were leaning against the Belvedere's handrail, sublime in His glory but with compassion for mankind. He noticed with pleasure in the mirror that reflected his new image that the relatives, one after another, were straggling out to the terrace. There they breathed in the slight breeze of a night of very low clouds, tinted ocher above the hill by the glare of lights shining at the University—possibly the floodlights in the stadium or the Patio of Columns—while they remarked on the disrespect of the person up above who, so close to death, was still playing records. It wasn't dance music, to be sure; but music is only played out of happiness. When they talked about dispatching the Soldier, with his air of authority, to demand greater solemnity in the presence of the deceased, a ship's siren made all of them forget what had perhaps stopped playing. They talked about pilots, buoys, and swells, and minute hands were synchronized on a bet because someone asserted that the light on the light-house was turning more slowly than the regulations allowed. Returning from his trip through the mirror, the man who was now lean turned toward the door that the others were using his stakes and planks to keep open, because, having been shut for so long, it tended to close by itself, pushed shut by the habit of its thick, studded hinges. Only two old ladies, their heads covered by white handkerchiefs, were left in the room, praying over the beads of a single rosary, so he slid his pistol over his hip, where he usually wore it, put his hand on the railing, and slowly walked down the spiral staircase, whose creaking steps had come to speak to him in the clear language of footfalls. He crossed the patio of the Academy of Style where, despite the dead neighbor, the girls were busily dressing the two dummies—one fat, the other thin—in cutout sheets of newsprint bristling with pins. The vision of the avenue at street level seemed so new to him that he hesitated before stepping over the threshold. Above, the Belvedere, its corner columns crowned with rosettes. Under the harsh light, the poplars painted wide shadows isolated one from another by the surrounding brightness of the sidewalk. After putting on his glasses, whose dark lenses—made for the sun, used at night—made him more hidden as he slipped from shadow to shadow, speeding up, sinking his face between his lapels whenever he walked under a light. The only money he had was that new bill, tossed to him as some kind of charity in the last house from which he'd been expelled, on the afternoon when a bullet-riddled column had saved him from death. It wasn't enough for him to make the trip to his father's tailor shop. Besides, everyone in Sancti-Spiritus would find out about his arrival: the veteran who sold fruit next to the Obelisk of the National Heroes knew him; the anise-bread seller knew him; the barbers who saw everyone pass by through the flutter of their gossipy scissors. He thought about eating. But at that early hour the cheap restaurants would be too full of people who would stare at him—and nothing was so fearful to him as a stare now that he had thrown himself into the city. Walking from shadow to shadow, he reached the end of the trees and passed into the world of columns. Columns with blue and white stripes, with railings connecting them: a double gallery of portals along that royal roadway whose Fountain of Neptune was adorned with tritons that looked like wild dogs pasted over with campaign posters. Following the paint smeared on the houses, he moved from ocher to ash, from green to mulberry, passing from the portal with a broken coat of arms over it to the portal adorned with filthy cornucopias. From the corners there stretched forward straight streets whose asphalt was tinged with a leaden blue in the light of street lamps that rocked gently in the breeze in a blur of bedazzled insects. There the parish church was sleeping, a plaster-cast Gothic structure—repainted so often that its fleurons looked as if they'd been dipped in molasses—with weeds sprouting from the roof tiles and grass growing on the awnings, across the street from the store that sold magnets, lightning-struck stones, and hands made of jet, used to protect children from illness and the evil eye. Beyond, there appeared a vine on top of a ruinous masonry wall, next to the vast tobacco warehouse asleep in the aromatic half-light. Under the arcades of an old Spanish palace lay beggars wrapped up in papers among tin cans and broken machinery, suffering bad dreams, asleep in their own urine. Hurrying, the hunted man went from column shadow to column shadow, knowing he was close to the market, where at this hour mountains of pumpkins, green plantains, and yellow ears of corn were piling up near cages through whose bars the turkeys would stretch their heads that looked like dusty tulips. Beyond that was the street of the pawn-brokers, always ablaze with light as if for a soirée, with their wicker chairs hung from the ceiling above a chaos of pendulum clocks, consoles, and dressers, from which would emerge, as if it had gone off course, the neck of some double bass or a polychrome vase. And, beyond the mannequins in bridal gowns and communion suits, beyond the bronze of the funeral parlor, where the napping watchman rested his head against a coffin, was the marble counter covered with fish scales standing among brass pots of bile, tripes, and shells. Even farther back stood the barbershop with the gold-framed mirrors. Taking a detour, he passed among the smells of polenta, jerked beef, pungent, pickled things, and piles of salt cod, in order to avoid the lights of the café with its steaming coffeepots at whose doors he had been arrested that night. Finally he reached the corner of a dark street where windows called in hushed voices, and raised a door knocker which, at that moment, was his only chance. Behind the door, Estrella's footsteps unhurriedly answered.

"What happened, did you lose your way?" she asked as she opened the door, looking him over with ironic curiosity while the sleepy dog, trained not to bark at strangers, merely sniffed at him. "I just got back from a trip," he said to explain to a person who had recently praised his expensive, flashy clothing why he was wearing a suit inappropriate to the season and a shirt that was wrinkled from being washed under the faucet on the terrace. "Sunglasses?" she teased, plucking them off with one finger and comically modeling them: "Everything's black. Is it a fad?" "I haven't eaten yet," he answered, looking toward the kitchen shadowed by the hanging branches of the pomegranate tree. The dog had stretched out at the far end of the patio, next to a mound of leftovers that was so

abundant there could be nothing left in the pots. Estrella brought a bottle that still contained some liquor. When he reached her door, the man had been
on the point of instantly entrusting himself to the only
person who could help him tonight. But now the alcohol he drank quickly made him consider his situ-
ation more calmly. He was hidden once again. The
house she'd closed off behind his back covered and
concealed him. There were many hours yet before
dawn. He had before him ample and propitious time.
He knew he could count on Estrella. But before saying
a word, he ought to create once again the climate of
intimacy his two weeks of despair had broken down.
She liked his slow and prolonged way of possessing
her. He took her by the hand, drawing her toward the
bed. "Wait," she said, putting out the light and sliding
in next to him after removing her lipstick with a
cleansing tissue and covering the statue of the Virgin
with a cloth. But he had fallen into a boundless bed.
The softness of the pillow after his having tossed and
turned on the worn-out straw mattress that had holes
in it so big his shoulder would go right through them;
the liquor, which left his body without bones, soft, as
if made of warm wax; the relief of putting down his
heavy pistol, which he put on top of his clothes; the
wide, hot breast next to his cheek; the woman's arms,
more lullaby now than incitement: it all made him
settle, slowly, delightfully, his arms and legs slack,
into the great lap of a sleep at long last possible . . .
When he opened his eyes the lights were turned back
on. Estrella, her back toward him, had just put on a
blouse with green ribbons on the collar. In the moon
of the mirror, she looked at him with more indiffer-

ence than spite. "Come here," he said. "You won't be able to," she answered, putting on her lipstick. Knowing it would be easier to get her to take her clothes off again than to take off her lipstick, he sat up on the edge of the bed and made a gesture of rage. He was not going to allow this woman he had possessed so many times, whose professional insensibility, he could say with masculine pride, he had overwhelmed, who had moaned with pleasure under his weight, look at him with a bored expression after having lain at his side, as if she were giving him up as a lost cause. Now she was opening the street door, calling in the cat, which in a silent jump abandoned the roof and began snooping around with a flick of its nervous tail. In the face of this indifference from a woman who always begged him to stay all night, the man exploded. How could his flesh be aflame at that moment when all of him was nothing but a vast clamor of hunger and fear! And now he was talking, breathlessly, needing to talk, to talk himself hoarse, after so much time without talking. Estrella closed the doors again. She huddled on the other side of the bed, listening with terrified attention. Suddenly, in a blaze of horrifying illumination, the implacable chain of events became real for her. Now she remembered the grisly newspaper photographs, although she had not seen in his stupid cowardice at that time the beginning of all this. The pictures now came back to her through his words, the origin of the fear, solitude, and hunger he had suffered in the distant house where they were now holding a wake for an old woman folded into her box, dead, with her guts still waiting for what he had stolen from her. As she absorbed the abominable im-

68

pact of what was said as a way to purge her mind of the men from the Inquisition, she heard the word she usually applied to herself when she openly bragged about what was plainly true, as if that word were being echoed back from a deep well. She did not remember when she had begun to like sitting on men's laps and smelling their shirts redolent of sweat and tobacco, knowing that tomorrow was secure when two hard arms sought each other out below her waist to hold her more tightly. She spoke of her body in the third person, as if, below her shoulder blades, it were an alien and energetic presence independently gifted with the powers that won her the solicitude and largess of men. That presence took instantaneous effect, as if through magic, inspiring prolonged diligence in men from different social classes, where life had other rhythms and other finalities. One man couldn't manage to explain what it was he studied; another was expecting something; yet another was longing for something. She was immobility and waiting, a known place among so many men of unknown domicile, who seemed to materialize when they turned the corner of her street and then just dissolved back into the city until the next time. Her head had a secondary role in the surprising life of a flesh that every man praised in similar terms, men rendered identical by the same gestures and appetites, a flesh she put on a pedestal and glorified as something unconquered, something that could only be possessed with great difficulty. She arrogated to herself the rights of indifference, frigidity, disdain—always demanding, although it might occur in silence when the bearing of the visitor or the insights of his arts seemed to justify an egoistic yielding of herself that inverted their roles, making the man act out the role of the woman casually possessed. Her body remained innocent of the notion of sin. She referred to It, separating it from herself, personifying it even more when she alluded to the place that constituted its center, as she might speak of a very valuable object, kept in another room in the house. "We sin with our heads," she had heard in a sermon which she had only half listened to once when she'd noticed that a few drops of holy water caused black stains to run from the lace of her mantilla, given to her as the genuine article. But her head had little to reproach her for, since she did what she did in accordance with the only work that would earn her decent wages. She was correct in her business dealings, reliable in her arrangements, generous where the needs of others were concerned or in the case of a woman like herself left destitute. Even the women on her street who had been married by the Church called her more a lady than some who pretended to chastity, using her as an example in their defamatory gossip. She bragged about her frankness, calling herself, for that very reason, by the most appropriate word. But now, as she learned about his fear, his hunger, his agonized solitude, the word became swollen with abjection. Now that she knew it was no longer five letters that came to her mouth, it was the ignoble Word, charged with purulence and lapidation; the insult that had resounded since time immemorial in jails, latrines, poorhouses, and vomitories. A sign, made to divert a threat of minor importance—a threat that if carried out would have had more impact on her comfort than her person—had made a whore of her. A whore, not because of the acts of her flesh, but because of the disloyal behavior that respectable people, women with only one man, usually attributed to those in her condition. This time she had sinned with her head, and these were the evils unleashed by her sin: the Word was shouted to her by voices from Hell, above the innocence of her body, shaken with horror . . . When the man, sweaty, panting, protested in louder and louder tones that he was sincere, told her about his prayers and entreaties, about the portentous news of God in his life, Estrella broke into sobs. It was he now who took her in his arms, laying her beside him. Before putting out the light, he removed her lipstick with a piece of cleansing tissue.

This time Estrella did not put on her lipstick. She cleansed her face with alcohol, her back turned toward him. Below her thick hair, bristling with combs, her eyes, now devoid of makeup, sank into her skin, which was lusterless, rather muddy, the complexion people have who grow up in charcoal smoke. From an armoire, she took out the black dress she wore to visit the Stations of the Cross during Holy Week and the dyed-black shoes she kept for sympathy visits and wakes. Chewing a crust he had dipped into the cold sauce left in a pot—all the leftovers had been thrown to the dog—the man felt an unexpected relief after possessing her. "I needed that even more than food," he thought. And he again described the house, emphasizing its details. The woman didn't know that distant part of town, through which she'd passed only a few times on her way back from the zoo, where she had been astounded by the exotic animals. Besides, everything outside her own parochial space was as alien to her as the other side of Havana Bay or beyond the ancient fortresses that guarded the port. She would talk about neighborhoods with names like Orfila, El Nazareno, or Palatino as if they were remote cities in whose streets a person might lose his way and wander for days. The routes she knew went from church to church, when she followed the Stations of the Cross during Holy Week. It was she who *was* visited, almost never visiting anyone herself. For that reason he had to paint a clear picture for her: at the intersection, it was the corner with the garden and the tall fence. Two floors: the entryway had a green awning and rocking chairs for children. There were white-painted statues standing in the beds of gladiolas and daisies. From the street she would be able to see the statues: a woman wearing a veil with an apple in her hand ("Eve?" she asked); the other one had a lance and a helmet, like a Soldier (in ancient times, women fought like men: her grandfather had told her so). And two lions, one on each side of the entrance, each with a black ring in its mouth (just like the ones on the monument that stood at the seashore, the one with the eagle on top of the columns). Visitors were not supposed to use the knocker (as they do here); instead, they were to pull a little chain that hung on the right side of the door. No one rang twice (as visitors do here); they were expected to wait a bit, every time. (Did he think she was totally ignorant of good manners?) She had to hand the letter to the Exalted Personage. And demand an answer, without letting herself be put off. In order to compromise him still further, she should pretend to know all about the Arrangement and speak in a courteous but firm tone, that of a woman ready to wait all night if necessary. Should the other grow impatient, she should adopt an ambiguous, ironic, disturbing tone, that of someone who knows a lot. If she met with resistance about being received; if the butler in white went out and came back, inviting her to come back tomorrow, she should talk about a *disaster*, without going into details: bad news opens doors. If the Exalted Personage had gone out, she should remain in the small waiting room decorated in the Spanish style. (Could she understand what he was saying about the carved chest, the two suits of armor, and the gauntlets on the hilts of the broadswords?) And if they didn't let her stay there, she should wait outside, next to the gate. Under the poplar there was a bench well known to those who came to solicit favors. Of the four corners at the intersection, it was the one with the garden and the tall fence . . . When Estrella turned toward him, her face clean, dressed in mourning, with no jewelry except a religious medal hanging around her neck on a thin chain, he almost laughed because she looked like one of the schoolgirls in the Academy of Style. "You look like a lady," he said, giving her the new bill he kept in his belt buckle. And, looking through the blinds, he watched her hail a taxi. It was eight o'clock. The people she was going to see dined late. Alone in the house, he felt secure, protected, owner of a night whose hours were bringing him closer to the end of his anguish. He got dressed slowly, smoothing out his suit as best as he could. Above the patio, the clouds, tinted purplish red by the city lights, thickened. Beyond, behind the pomegranate tree, was the dining room with the empty cupboard and its plaid oilcloth, while on the walls there were plates decorated with gondolas, castles, cats playing with balls of yarn, Neapolitan bays, and horseshoes resting on roses. He drank what liquor was left in the bottle, repeating to himself the text of the letter he had written, for want of better stationery, on one of those sheets of lined paper sold everywhere with two envelopes—in case the address gets smudged on the first. He wanted to do something to turn circumstances to his favor, praying that the addressee be in the house, that his emissary be received immediately, and that she return with news that would make him a free man. He took out the little book with the Cross of Calatrava on it, which he carried in his pocket as a good-luck charm. He went down on his knees before the statue of Saint Joseph decorated with rosaries, faintly illuminated by a single candle, reciting in a low voice the prayer to the Mediator between God and miserable sinners: "Most powerful patron and advocate, chosen, like Moses, by God not to guard a material ark but to watch over the true Ark of the Testament, Mary, in whose most pure womb the supreme lawgiver, Jesus Christ, took on human flesh . . ." When he finished, he wasn't sure whether he had counted nine or ten prayers, so he made himself recite eleven more. But someone started knocking at the door—one of Estrella's clients, no doubt—so he put out all the lights and crouched in the darkness, carefully listening to the noises in the street, where with each passing moment the commercial traffic converging on the market grew heavier and heavier. He slept a bit; or perhaps not; but the architect's triangle that sought out his hand could only have come to him during a very short nap, with his body braced uncomfortably against the wall. The triangle did not exist. Several trucks passed. And after a long wait, when his confidence was becoming clouded with impatience, voices raised in a harsh argument in front of the house made him leap up with a start. Estrella was trying to calm down a man who was shouting at her in sarcastic tones, loud enough for the passersby, whom he called on to be witnesses, to hear him. The lock made a noise, and the woman came running in, waving the new bill he had given her to pay the taxi fare. "The taxi driver says it's fake. And I haven't got any . . ." Now the knocker was banging on the door, echoing strongly through the rooms in the back. "He says the bills with the General with the sleepy eyes on them are no good. I'm broke. I had to pay the rent today." The man on the run took the bill and started to examine it, stupefied, stretching it against the light, turning it over, looking at it again and again, while the man outside kept up his shouting and joking. "I never make any trouble," whined Estrella. "I just mind my own business." A policeman slowly approached the door, where the man was still pounding the knocker. "Get out. I'll take care of this," said the woman, pointing toward the room where he'd prayed to Saint Joseph: a window led to a vacant lot. As he returned to the shadows, the door opened again and a confused dialogue began. The taxi driver, calm now, had accepted her apology and was excusing himself for having made such a fuss, telling how he'd gotten stuck with coun-

76

terfeit money that had been passed at night when it was easier to fool people. Then there was whispering and laughter. And, suddenly, Estrella's voice, exaggeratedly loud, so it could be heard on the other side of the patio. "I'm telling you, honey, there's no one here. Go inside and look if you want." Whipped by the warning, the man on the run slipped one leg over the windowsill and jumped into the darkness. He fell, slipping over a pile of wet papers mixed up with rotten fruit, feathers, oyster shells—refuse from the market, where tomorrow, after the dogs were finished, the vultures would be scratching around. His fatigue was suddenly so great that he remained there for a while, immobile among cold fruit skins and fish scales, unable to make up his mind to go. Tossed from above, a burning cigarette butt struck his hand. It was an unusual butt, made of country-style corn paper, the kind very few people use. The pain snapped him out of his inertia, and he stood up, uncertain which way to go. He felt for his sunglasses: he had left them behind on a woven wicker table next to Estrella's bed. The headlights of a car that turned the corner stretched his shadow the length of the wall.

Now he worked to clean up his blue suit at the old fountain, which had been a watering place for horses and mules in the days when the big carts came down to the city early in the evening to the rhythm of the tired nodding of little bells. Lacking a brush, he rubbed the fabric with a handful of straw he'd moistened in the water, which was still warm from the sun. But suddenly it seemed to him that two workers were observing him too closely. He had nothing to fear from such people, but he still moved away, down a street where cabbage leaves had fallen into the gutter and pieces of fruit were trampled into the sewer grating. It was a long distance to the House of the Arrangement, even without taking a roundabout route. He measured it out mentally in terms of trees, because he needed shadows, and in terms of hills, because of his despair at their height, as if he were following an interminable path through the wilderness. He was about to knock at Estrella's door to make her appear, but he remembered that when she was with someone she would put out all the lights in the front of the house and refuse to answer the door. He also knew that some of her customers, though they might return later if they thought she was shopping or doing errands, would think twice before lying in sheets still warm from another man. Besides, he couldn't be sure the woman could get rid of the taxi driver that quickly; after all, the man might take advantage of what had been offered to him in payment and stay until after midnight. Therefore, he had to get *there* as soon as possible, and find out, finally find out once and for all, without delays or evasions, if tomorrow the night that had lasted so long would finally come to an end. He was asking for so little: a visa, some money, and people—that most of all, People!—to be around him at the last moment. The one to whom he'd speak now was the Man from the National Palace. He had relieved the Man of a feared adversary by means of an exploding book he'd sent through the mail. He had to find a thick book, strongly bound, within whose pages a kind of grave could be carved—*Anthology of Orators: From Demosthenes to Castelar*, a Madrid edition from the beginning of the century. The infernal device was placed very neatly between Cicero and Gambetta. Later, the man who'd actually doctored the tome had been picked up with the others, without revealing anything—"singing" they called it. Only he—a survivor walking between the metal curtains of

79

a tortuous street of closed stores—knew the secret of what had been sent. As proof, he had hidden the receipt for the certified package, which he'd mailed under a false name. He would remind the Man from the National Palace—if it was necessary; he would threaten to send his copy to the newspapers with a long letter of explanation; he would force the Man from the National Palace to act without delay. "Stay right where you are and wait," he'd been told. But the wait had gone on too long, and a death that happened to cross his path had finally driven him from the Belvedere. Just then he thought that it is indeed an ill wind that turns none to good. When the old lady who had once nourished him with the milk of her breasts died, she had done him a final good deed, one he could never repay . . . He hurried on, his courage renewed, thinking that he had been stupid to send Estrella to ask for what he, more than anyone, had the right to demand. He turned onto the wide avenue with its double row of trees guarded by the marble statue of the Spanish King with his wig, Order of the Golden Fleece, and velvet costume. He passed columns of a grand era that stood like the solitary remains of an ancient triumph, especially if compared to the neighboring smeared orange and blue columns or the flowers and other bizarre ideas of this pastry-shop, half-breed architecture. He passed in front of the incredibly high Gothic spire whose supporting arches opened over a store that sold shells and amulets for black rites, and crossing through the portal of the Grand Lodge, he swerved away from the sickle emblems of the Party's central office, where the lights were still burning because of some cell meeting. Hurrying, he remembered how he had also rejected the Party, soon after arriving from Sancti-Spiritus, and used the gesture of crossing himself as he passed a statue of the Virgin in a building entrance as an excuse. Just ahead stood the severe palings of the fence around the botanical garden, with its flower beds labeled with Latin terms, trees sick with orchids; its *Victoria regias* blooming over sleeping waters, among gigantic malanga vines speckled with the cold light of the street lamps. On the street-sided hill behind, tinged black over reddish clouds, rose the prison, built directly opposite the ancient Spanish fortress. It was similar to those erected—under orders from the Champion of Catholicism—in these islands by an Italian military architect, enormously ingenious at hiding dungeons, corridors, and secret cells in the entrails of the stone. The fugitive trembled when he remembered that it was there—near the fourth watchtower, from whose embrasure so many screams had emanated— where, not so long before, his most irreplaceable flesh had recoiled atrociously before the threat of torture. Since the trees were getting thicker, he sought their shadows to free himself from the abominable memory. He stopped, breathless, at the foot of the hill of the University, under whose lights the loudspeakers were blaring. The lights, unusual at that hour, reminded him of the drama productions put on from time to time in the Patio of Columns, where hundreds of spectators came to watch some tragedy acted by literature students dressed up as Messengers, Guards, and Heroes. The man on the run measured in that instant how short the journey had been from that building of high rows of columns and its HOC ERAT IN

81

votis that could be read from a distance under allegories of Knowledge, to the expiatory, dark fortress where he'd been made to confess abjectly—"to sing," as they called it—what he'd learned from men met, ill met, in the halls of the University. The loudspeakers bellowed in a different key about the sons of Atreus, and the Chorus bellowed a strophe that stopped the fugitive in his tracks at the crest of a bare hill, bristling with hawthorn bushes: *The curses are being fulfilled; Those under the earth are alive; Men long dead draw blood from their murderers to answer blood.* The breeze, changing direction, carried the words away. The man sat on the curb, protected by a thick-topped poplar that was dropping black seeds on the cement which its roots were pushing up. Everything had been just, heroic, and sublime in the beginning: the houses they'd blown up during the night; the dignitaries shot down in the streets; the automobiles that disappeared as if swallowed by the earth; the explosives that were stored at home, among clothes perfumed with bunches of sweet basil—next to the pamphlets carried in bakery baskets or in cases of beer whose bottles had been cut so that only the necks remained. It was a time when death sentences were passed from afar, a time for modest valor, a time for putting your life on the line. It was a time for dazzling executions carried out by an emissary wearing an implacable smile, executions that took place when the guilty party opened a book or a Christmas present wrapped in paper decorated with mistletoe and bells. It was the time of the Tribunal . . .

(. . . although I tried to cover it up, to silence it, I have it before me, always before me; after months of a forgetting that was not a forgetting—when I found myself right back in that afternoon, I shook my head violently, trying to shuffle the images, like a child who sees his parents' bodies enveloped in filthy ideas; after many days have gone by, it is still the odor of rotten water under the roses forgotten in their carnelian vases; the lights turned on after sunset has closed the arcades of that long, too long, gallery of awnings; the heat of the roof, the Venetian mirror with its beveled edges, and, from above, the noise of the music box when the breeze shakes the crystal pendants that drape the lamp with an icy fringe. A few drops of rain were falling as we entered, and, sure enough, the monk

83

on the Swiss barometer is praying in his prie-dieu with his hood halfway off, since a few drops of rain fell as we were entering. We all know what will be said here; we all know that the already loaded weapons behind the screen will be used. Nevertheless, this ceremony is thought necessary so we can go through with it and have steadier hands when we're finished. These are the times of the Tribunal. I hear the warbling of the birds in their cage with its gilt bars, filigreed domes, and glass doors, and I see the turtles slowly yawning, raising their heads above the pool of turbid water. Everything takes on enormous importance in that instant of suspended time—still suspended, as if everything that was to take place afterward had already happened. The law-school people, who will act as judges, enter and sit down behind the table, and then the accused enters, smoking a good cigar, whose ash he tries not to lose, in a show of calm contradicted by his pallor and his uncertainty about where to put his legs. The Prosecutor, who has put on a dark tie though everyone else is in shirtsleeves, is now talking about the attempt on the Chancellor's life: the routes had been studied, the place for the attack was chosen, the men, with open or closed newspapers, were at their posts pointing to the best escape route; the men who transformed automobiles with their acetylene torches, their spray guns, and their quick-drying paints would return a completely unknown car that very night. It was then that the imaginative ones proposed the tunnel. And so great was the desire to get it all over with—to blow up the man and all his dignitaries—that they began to dig a tunnel from the

84

riverbank toward the family mausoleum, whose white angel had his wide wings spread open and his hands clasped in prayer. We would set the charges, set them to explode when someone pronounced the panegyric, under the last empty vault. We worked at night, sinking a little deeper each time into the clayish soil that stank of the sewer. When we realized, because we were pounding the base with our picks, that we were under the outer walls of the cemetery, the stench was so terrible that some of the diggers fainted and had to be revived by the medical students with concoctions prepared by the pharmacy students. The horrible work shift lasted until dawn, when the first roosters, those belonging to the fishermen, put an end to that labor of darkness, which slowly lengthened its path under crosses and chapels, toward the white angel, which served as a guide ... "Defend yourself!" I shout, when the Prosecutor points to the Informer, whose words had spoiled that great work and cost us several lives. "Defend yourself!" everyone shouts, demanding to know his unknown motive, if he suffered intolerable coercion, their impossible surprise that the men could have left their weapons on the bed in the room with screens—the shovels inert at the foot of the thickest trunk. But, overwhelmed, the man shrugs his shoulders, defeated beforehand, and again accepts what we all knew . . . The word "death" is pronounced. And after it is spoken, after this word which is an end, after this word which is the antithesis of creation, the silence grows. A silence that already belongs to the time *afterwards*, to what has already ceased to be; premonition and movement that already know about the monkey wrench tossed into the heart of the machinery, about the earth that will fall on the still warm immobility of what has been stopped. The body present—present but already absent—detaches a watch from his wrist slowly because he already knows himself to be beyond time; he winds it out of habit with the thumb and index finger of his right hand; he places it on the table, leaving it to someone else, and he looks for the last time at the hands of an hour that for him will never end. It is the body that amazed me in the stadium showers, when he came in from being acclaimed, sweaty, filthy with scratches, smelling like an animal, and the padding that had covered the fur on his back fell off. I wanted those back muscles that moved so smoothly over his bones for myself; I wanted that stomach that narrowed between his hips until they squeezed into blackness; I wanted those legs made longer by jumping that ran toward the water under a chest that had just released its surplus of energy in singing and shouting. And they were hideous words as he lathered his head, proclaiming that he still had a yen for women, music, liquor. In my province, the intellectuals—assiduous conversationalists at the tailor shop, contemplators of the fountain in whose shadow the poet Heredia had meditated—had declared muscles stupid and only the spirit grand. I envied that flesh when it lived among us, reduced to its most masculine dimensions, unaltered by its own excesses, lifted by the pole, vaulting over obstacles, hurling the javelins of ancient warriors. Now his miserable shoulders sagged before the Judges, virtually counting their last heartbeats. And we have to raise

86

our hands to pass sentence. There are two, five, I don't know how many hands. Mine remains inert, hanging, seeking a pretext not to rise above the back of a dog that wags its tail at the foot of my chair. "Defend yourself!" I say again in a voice so low that no one hears me. And, as it waits for all the others, my elbow finally moves, raising cowardly fingers to the same level as those of the others. Everyone embraces the sentenced man without looking him in the eye. The executioners retrieve their weapons. And, a short time later, a shot is fired at the foot of the tree with the thickest trunk. I am astounded, now, in the face of what lies there, at how simple it is to cut short an existence. Everything seems natural: what once moved has stopped moving; his voice was silenced in a mouthful of blood that looks like a compact piece of enamelwork, covering his unshaven chin; everything that could be felt has been felt, and immobility has only broken a cycle of reiterations. "It had to be done," they all say, their consciences in dialogue, looking for themselves in History. And they disperse into the night, without having to hide any longer or to distrust the shadows, because times have changed, repeating in louder and louder tones that *it* had been necessary so that we could be pure as we enter into the times that have changed. And the pitch of their voices rises, the farther away from them the body lies ... The birds sleep under the filigree domes; the turtles remain motionless, lifting their heads out of the turbid pond. The monk in the Swiss barometer has pushed back his hood—I remember—because a few drops of rain fell and were quickly absorbed by the dried-out roof tiles. Above the tree with the thickest trunk, the flies pause, looking for the bullets that went all the way through. On one of the branches, a frog croaks with the dry song of a nocturnal bird. Those were the times of the Tribunal . . .)

. . . the times of the Tribunal, well, it was two or three years ago that exasperation unleashed terror in broad daylight. The Tribunal passed sentence and loosed the vengeful, implacable Furies against the weak and the informers. But after the necessary, the just, the heroic, after the times of the Tribunal, came the time of looting. Exempt from reprisals, the malcontents gave themselves over to taking chances, which they did in armed groups that trafficked in violence, proposing plans and extorting rewards. They would unleash the Furies in broad daylight, this time to the advantage of this or that politico. Even the police fled when they appeared. They were feared, and their powerful protectors knew how to make holes in prison walls. They still asserted that this was just and necessary; but whenever the man ejected from the Belvedere, the man now under sentence, returned from a job, he had to drink himself insensible in order to go on believing that what he'd done had actually been just and necessary. A price had been placed on the shedding of blood, even though that price was quoted in the language of revolution. And when he remembered how the expression "undercover man" was used in those days, the man seated on the curb clenched the hand that would have voted for the death sentence. How miserable his shoulders felt, as they sank in the shadow of the poplars, how fearful he was of seeing the eyes of the executioners light up in the night . . . (Their weapons are loaded and waiting somewhere, like those that rested in that bed, behind the screen, their triggers, butts, muzzles all ready, loaded even before the sentence was pronounced. "Defend yourself," I said. But I spoke without wanting to be heard. I spoke to myself; so I could say to myself that I had spoken. I've come to wonder now if I spoke or if the echo of what was spoken by the others echoed in me. And that walk, avoiding his eyes, toward the thickest trunk, which was then shedding its bark—I remember—just like this one that leaves a smell like bitter almonds on my fingernails. On one of its branches a frog sang, just as one did on that afternoon—when I felt authorized to sit at the right hand of the Lord . . .) He was disgusted, sick to his stomach over all he'd lived since then; longing to drag himself to the foot of a confessional in order to shout that nothing had been necessary, to vomit all his guilt so that exceptional punishments would be meted out to him, the most terrible the Church had ever instituted. He took satisfaction in the idea that such punishment could exist for anyone who could pour out abominations like his. He threw himself facedown on the roots of the poplar—so hard that his teeth, after clamping on something, brought the taste of his blood to his mouth—when he saw two men slowly walking down the hill toward the shadows that protected him. "A drunk," said the older man bending over slightly. "Maybe he died from a heart attack," opined the one who didn't want to look. "They'll pick him up tomorrow." They walked off toward the avenue. For them as well, death was something easy. A stiff corpse becomes a thing to be taken or brought; something bothersome because it weighs a lot and is hard to carry, something that—as a matter of *form*—just can't be left in the street like that. It looks like a person, and because of its shape it evokes a certain period of time that should end below the roots and not above them. "They'll pick him up tomorrow," repeated the older man, already far away, as if to excuse himself from having to notify the authorities. The fugitive got up, shaking off the red ants that were running up his sleeves. Their bites spurred him to start walking. He stopped quite soon to make sure that those footsteps echoing on the opposite sidewalk were his own. The breeze changed from south to north and again carried with it the bellow of the loudspeakers, with their women's choruses, among which stood out, because of its high pitch, the voice of a female pharmacy student he knew: *Return quickly to the vestibule to finish with the second matter, just as you have done with the first.* And a man answered: *Have no fear, we shall know how to end the affair. But soon: by whatever road you*

91

choose! howled some Electra insistently. The voice was right. It was necessary to hurry and get there as soon as possible, by any road. Nor had that part about "we shall know how to end the affair" spoken by the other voice been an evil omen . . . Before him the avenue, where various Presidents, with thick bronze frock coats, standing on granite pedestals, were sculpted in heroic size above the ice-cream vendors, who were ringing their viaticum bells, descended to the sea covered over by clouds palpitating with distant flashes of lightning. Here he'd have to stay close to the houses because the palm trees, whose tops were higher than the highest streetlight, cast no shadow. The fugitive reached the obscure street with the sad café whose green wood columns were a squalid imitation of the Tuscan order, and in long strides he reached the corner where the House of the Arrangement, its walls gone, had been reduced to pillars standing on a marble floor covered with rocks, beams, and chunks of stucco chipped off the ceilings. The gates and the lions that bit iron rings had been taken away. A wheelbarrow path leading upward crossed the grand salon to end at a pantry where several shovels jutted out of a pile of shapeless stones. Next to the wrought-iron railing with its Andalusian tracery, the statue of the goddess Pomona from the garden had been laid on its back, with base and pedestal in the grass spattered with plaster from the moldings. A dog was sleeping under the sign painted in thick brush-strokes on a broken barrel:

FREE RUBBLE

Only a wall of the back room remained; a wheelbarrow lay on its side in the spot where the Spanish desk
had stood—it had amused him so much that other
time because of its inlaid pictures of straw dummies
being tossed in blankets during carnival and of Madrid riffraff vaulting over bulls. It was difficult to re-
construct the office's furnishings mentally: the table
was decorated with a dry inkwell, bronze eagles, and
blotters set in embossed leather. But as he sat there
in that corner, protected from street light, the moment
of the fissure became very real to him. Until that moment, the terrible work of the squad had required
fearlessness, forgetting himself, and sacred fury. They
had shown him how to counterfeit license plates, to
carry dynamite, to saw off shotgun barrels, to make

93

shells with two parts birdshot to one part buckshot; he'd learned about codes and cryptography by using the word "triangle"—it had no repeated letters—and rearranging the letters in seemingly disordered strings that corresponded to a secret order; he learned how to decipher the secret language of newspaper articles. They had sunk their picks into the clay that stank of sewers and the rot of coffins; in that tunnel they dug beneath the cemetery of the solemn poor in order to reach the Chancellor's dome and blow up all those they hated. "Good and dead, the dog," they would say bitterly in those days, as they watched hasty funerals pass among the tombs, the fearful mourners nervously glancing toward the cypress trunks. "Good and dead, the dog," he would repeat, looking at the black-framed obituary page in the newspaper, whose *Requiescat in pace* seemed too forgiving to him . . . And then one day it was his turn to shoot someone; it took place on the wide avenue of the Bronze Presidents. Ordering his driver to take the port road so he could enjoy the morning breeze, the victim tapped out a song on the green car door. A ruby glittered on his ring finger. The pursuers pulled up at just the right speed, raising their weapons from the car floor smoothly, without getting in one another's way. "Take off the safety," the man on his right advised him, aware that he was new to this work. The back of the victim's neck was soon so close that they could have counted his acne scars. Then he became a profile, a horrified face, two begging eyes, a howl, and shots. With a clatter of metal, the bullet-ridden car slammed against one of the galley prows that flanked the monument to the heroic Martyrs, while the pursuers

turned onto a cross street. "Good and dead, the dog."
But that night he'd still had to drink until he was in
a stupor and fell in a daze into Estrella's bed in order
to forget that acne-scarred neck which had been there,
just beyond his weapon—almost within reach of his
hand. Soon after, when he found out that someone
had benefited from that death, he'd been plagued by
doubts, which were soon silenced by those around him
who skillfully used the Words that justified everything. "The revolution," they said, "is not over yet."
And step by step, dragged along by his increasingly
active hands, he passed into the bureaucracy of horror. First there was fury, as he swore to avenge those
who had fallen, thinking HOC ERAT IN VOTIS as he contemplated the corpses of the condemned; but soon it
became a profession of easy money and protection in
high places. And one morning, sitting in front of the
desk with its Goya-inspired marquetry, he had accepted a fee for masterminding the preparation of a
certain *Anthology of Orators* and sending it through
the mail. When he was arrested the next day, near the
market café where he always went after leaving Estrella's house, he realized that the police were acting
out of mere suspicion, that they had no hard evidence,
since the postal receipt was safely hidden and the pre-
parer had fled the city when he found out that the
book had in fact exploded in the hands of the man to
whom it had been sent. And, as for the Exalted Personage, he was the person most interested in keeping
things quiet . . . He remembered going over the drawbridge to the fortress; the black dungeons from whose
walls rusty chains still hung; the walk along corridors
and past cells where the lights were never turned off

in order to keep the men stretched out on the canvas and metal cots from coming together on the floor like beasts. And after two days of being forgotten, without food—without alcohol, after having drunk so much for months—there had been the light in his face, hands wielding billy clubs, voices talking about drilling his teeth right down to the roots, and other voices talking about beating his testicles. The idea of an assault on his sex was intolerable to him, beyond all right, beyond all power. He had killed, but he hadn't castrated. And now they were going to mutilate him, cut him off from himself, dry him out, depriving him of the axis where his body had its coat of arms, his most intimate pride, the infallibility of whose autonomous power he had boasted of. Within a few minutes, he would be set on the road to old age, deprived of future pleasures, of possessing innumerable women, dead for other flesh. His reality fell to pieces, ripped open, under the lights burning above his face like those in an operating room, with the sound of voices coming ever nearer— horrifyingly amplified by the resonance of that chamber with its low parapet—talking about hurting the thing he was so proud of, talking about emasculating him, ruining him, castrating him. The hands that approached his grimace, the sweat on his limbs, intensified his fear of a pain that would have hurt him less in another part of his body. Now everything would collapse; a death before dying, which he'd have to bear for interminable days without embraces, bearing the weight of his own cadaver. The first bite of the pincers drew such a long and desolate animal howl out of him that the others, calling him a coward, silenced him with a punch. And when he again felt the metal against his shrunken skin, he called out for his mother with a hoarse wail that turned into a death rattle and sob in the deepest part of his throat. And, with his eyes fixed on the lights that filled his pupils with their incandescent circles, clutching his sex as if he were recovering it, holding it close and reintegrating it into his flesh, he began to talk. He told them whatever they wanted to hear; he explained the recent attacks, and depicted himself as an apprentice, an extra, in order to lessen his own guilt; he listed the names of those who at that moment were sleeping on the couches in a certain villa in the suburbs or drinking and dealing cards at a long table in the dining room with their pistols hung over the backs of their chairs. Filled to overflowing with so much information, so many revelations, the questioners believed him when he said he knew nothing about the preparation and mailing of the book that had caused two deaths, attributing the work to the collective activity of his team. And when the naked man, hanging on to his sex, declared that he knew no more, they returned him to his cell with a cigarette as reward. Once again he was locked up, with the footsteps in the corridor and the terrible fear that it would start all over again. At dawn, he sent a message to the warden, asking that notice of his imprisonment be sent to the Man from the National Palace. Half an hour later he was set free by an order that came from the personal secretary . . . He crossed the drawbridge and slowly walked down the hill from the fortress, excited after that passage through hell at the awakening streets. It was like the beginning of a convalescence; a return to the world of men. He wasn't even hungry, had not the slightest

97

desire to walk up to the big mahogany bars where the early-morning drinkers were pouring out the first drops of liquor, before tasting it, as an offering to the souls of the dead. In the softly clouded light, the poplars chirped with all their feathers. The spire on the Sacred Heart Church, a blurred opalescent whiteness, raised its marble Virgin above the countrified dome of San Nicolás, where at that time elderly black women with graying hair and many rosaries were attending Mass, fulfilling vows made to the Nazarene by wearing violet sackcloth fastened with a yellow badge. And the cupolas of flesh-colored mosaics, the gilt crosses, and the coppery belfries of the Carmen, the San Francisco, and Las Mercedes were glittering in the morning air, in the awakening of the terraces edged with balusters where the washerwomen hung out their clothes. Behind them, the view of the sea was so overpowering that the fishing boats seemed to be sailing above the roofs. The freed man went to his room, enjoying the coolness of the portals, the smell of the fruit on the scales, the smoke of the coffee ovens—discovering, much as someone who comes home from the hospital discovers, the unctuous quality of butter, the crunch of whole-wheat bread, the gentle splendor of honey. He slept until noon, when he was awakened by newsboys hawking a special edition. The papers showed bodies lying on a sidewalk he knew only too well, puddles of blood among turned-over furniture, men dying on operating tables, and some windows—in the kitchen and the pantry—through which a few had leaped into a gully. That same afternoon, as he made his way to the house of the Exalted Personage—the house that now only had walls of air—he found protection just in time behind a column and saved himself from a barrage of bullets fired from a black car whose license plates were covered by a tangle of streamers. After all, it was carnival time.

The dog woke up and, looking toward the shadows above, began to bark, not furiously but monotonously, one bark after another, interrupted by pauses in which he spun around searching for the unreachable fleas in his skinny tail. The man on the run got up heavily and walked down the wheelbarrow path, entering through the collapsed ceiling into the salon, where, dirty and faded, the syrinxes and tambourines of a Pompeian allegory were still visible. On the threshold without a door, the dog waited for him, barking reluctantly. "I'm not worth the trouble of a bite," thought the man, crossing the garden bristling with stakes. After sinking ankle-deep into some mud encrusted with plaster, he reached the street. The idea of retracing his route across the city, along the tree- and column-lined streets, in order to reach Estrella's far-off house was unthinkable. His fatigue went beyond fatigue. It was a dense stupor in which all his limbs moved as if they were being dragged along by an outside force. He had resigned himself to giving up the fight, to stopping once and for all and just waiting for the worst; and yet he went on walking with no particular goal, from sidewalk to sidewalk, lost on the street he knew best. He could have dropped at the foot of that tree, if it hadn't been for those obstinate, muffled barks that followed next to his ankles. He remembered some vacant lots among whose weeds he could hide and sleep. But they were too far away for his fatigue. The only money he had was the counterfeit bill Estrella had given back to him, which would be rejected everywhere and provoke dangerous arguments. His own apartment was being watched by *the others*. In cheap hotels, it was necessary to pay in advance; his appearance was too lamentable for him to walk into the big hotels with the notion of running out without paying the bill the next day. Why didn't men today have that ancient option of "claiming sanctuary" spoken of in a book on the Gothic? Oh, Jesus! If at least your Houses were open on this unending night so I could fall down on their paving stones in the peace of the naves, and groan and free myself of all that I have hidden in my heart! . . . Oh, if I could only lie face-down on the cold floor, with this stony weight I'm dragging—my cheek against the cold stone, my hands open over the cold stone; my fever gone, and my thirst, and this heat that burns my temples—all relieved by the coldness of the stone! . . .

A church was lit up in the night, surrounded by ficus and palms; the fleurons on its slender steeple gleamed in the night. Its stained-glass windows were ablaze; the purples and the greens of the greater rose window flashed. And, suddenly, the doors of the nave swung open, and there appeared the path of red carpets that would lead the wedding party to the altar, resplendent with candles. The man on the run slowly approached the House that seemed to offer itself to him; he passed under the ogee of one of the lateral doors and stopped, dazzled, at the foot of a pillar whose stone was redolent of incense. His hands sought out the coolness of the holy water, bringing it to his forehead and mouth. An organ quietly sounded, as if someone were trying out its higher registers. There, standing on a lace-covered altar, was the Cross, clearly delineated by the body of Christ. So great was the man's shock when confronted by the reality that had materialized because of his plea that his lips could not whisper the prayers he'd learned in his little book. He could only look, stare fixedly at what for him was burning outside the night of fear. He advanced from pillar to pillar— as before he'd gone from tree to tree—timidly approaching, step by step, the Table of the Eucharist. Each stopping place, each station, freed him from a mantle of horrors. He would stop, relieved, delighted to breathe in the air smelling of melted wax, of the varnish used in the recent restoration of a Last Supper. He rested his fingers on the railing of the pulpit, on the wood of a confessional, with the feeling that he was touching a precious substance. For the first time, he knew—he felt—what a church could be, bearing his ever more bearable flesh along the mystic ark toward Christ, who had bled because of His nails and the thorns in His crown, above altar cloths covered with flowers . . . "Are you a guest?" asked a quiet voice behind him. "I am," he answered without turning around, hearing muffled footsteps fade away. But, behind him, a great murmur, coming first from the atrium, grew louder and louder as it reached the vaults. He was close to the sacristy when he noticed that sound, as if he'd suddenly recovered his hearing after a vertiginous ascent to the heights of the universe. Women wearing light-colored dresses came in, men in full-dress suits, little girls carrying bouquets: people who did not look at him, who did not see him, all moving under the lights, a sunflower of ribbons and flounces. The man on the run understood why the naves had been illuminated that night: now the bride would come, grand marches would be played, dowries would be exchanged, rings would be put on, and the sanctuary, empty again, would return to the shadows. When everything was over, he would find, at long last, someone who would want to listen to him. This House was asylum and help. The parish priest, no doubt, would know the Personage whose house, now being demolished, was so near. After hearing the abominable truths that would have to come from his mouth—he would tell all, everything, as one should when speaking to Him from whom nothing can be hidden—he would perhaps get help from his confessor. The organ rang out in epithalamic tones, and there was a great movement of the procession toward the altar. Wrapped in the half-light of a side chapel, the man on the run watched the ceremony as if in a dream, following the movements of the officiant. The rites and readings seemed interminable to him, even though he told himself a thousand times that his impatience was sacrilegious, and that he had no right to an opinion about what was happening under the nails in the Cross. The organ pipes sang out again in their triumphal bellowing. And then came the dispersion of people who took all too long to leave. The lights began to go out; the shadows returned to the central nave, while, beyond, the high doors were closing. Some diligent silhouettes bent down to roll up the carpets, while others took down decorations and straightened out the benches once again. When those people had finally left, all was silent: a great silence glittering with candles that partially illuminated the holy paintings: Christ in the Epiphany, the Bleeding

Christ, and a Last Supper, whose too fresh varnish was mottled with reflections . . . The man waited for a long time without daring to enter the sacristy, where a presence revealed itself in the noise of closing armoires and the light clatter of metallic objects. But, suddenly, the corpulent outline of the parish priest materialized in the door frame, dressed in a light-colored soutane. "Who's there?" he asked in a loud voice, as he picked up a heavy candlestick. The man on the run came out of the shadows, weighed down by the unforeseen idea that he might be taken for a thief. As if trying to explain himself, he showed the book with the Cross of Calatrava on it. The priest looked at it suspiciously, making a slightly defensive gesture. Someone was trying to talk to him now, down on his knees, clutching the dark little book in his tense hands. But his sobs interrupted his sentences, which made no sense anyway and always returned to the same ideas of guilt and self-abomination. Shocked, the priest listened without trying to understand that hoarse voice, which broke down in weeping and choking, accusing itself of obscure crimes and infernal perpetrations. He had professional experience with the crises of people who could stand for an entire day with their arms crossed at the foot of the Virgin of Sorrows, demanding for themselves the daggers she bore in her wounds; or others who would describe their obsessions as if they had lived them, retelling them as soon as they'd been granted absolution—taking confession every morning in a different church just to tell the same things; or those others who walked on their knees on the church floor, several scapularies hanging from their chests, irritatingly eager to hold up the poles in processions—putting their shoulder to the wheel for the Nazarene, with excessive displays of fervor. They were the same ones who, when they became ill, would go to the False Virgins, the saints with black faces, calling them by barbarous names. "Tomorrow," he said, with just those parishioners in mind. "Tomorrow. Come to confession tomorrow." And the more the man insisted, the more rapidly he repeated "Tomorrow, tomorrow, tomorrow, tomorrow," accentuated by an impatience that was turning into anger. His eyes suddenly fixed on the small book with the Cross of Calatrava on it which the kneeling man had dropped to the floor: despite the imprimatur they carried in due and proper form, books like this were the kind sold in witchcraft shops along with dolls dressed in red, bells sacrilegiously marked JHS, and clay heads with seashell eyes. The prayers were good, but those who recited them had their minds set on the heresies of witch doctors, asking for things that could not be requested in a church. Rage reddened the priest's face. With a vigorous hand he pulled the man, who went on crying, up from the floor and led him firmly through the sacristy with its chests to the rear door, which he blocked with his wide body. "Tomorrow," he said for the last time, softening his tone. "And remember that you must fast; eat nothing after twelve." Several turns of the lock clicked behind the door, which was then secured by a bar. In the twinkling of an eye, all the lights on the façade went out, the fleurons became dark, and the church became one with the shadows of the ficus and palm trees, suddenly shaken by a wind that promised rain. "Eat nothing after twelve."

105

Walking again, staggering, tripping over everything, hurt by the cracks in the sidewalk, by the roots, by a stone put where his foot would hit it. One final idea: the candles must still be lit, there, next to the old lady's coffin. And they would be burning until dawn, in a place where they'd already seen him, where no new faces would be appearing. Go up the stairs, again shake hands with the relatives, repeat the "Please accept my sincerest sympathies," and fall onto the mattress in the Belvedere without worrying about the people shoving on the inside. They wouldn't bother him until after the burial. The house was not far away, since this was the street with the saddlery that had the coach in it, the visiting-card printing shop. He was hurrying, making a renewed effort, when two nervous hands grabbed him from behind by the elbows. A voice he knew spoke above the back of his neck, which was ready to receive the blade. "I want to embrace a real man," said the Scholarship Student, releasing him so he could stagger toward him. And, drunk, imitating admiration by bobbing his head around, he spoke of raising a monument to the glory of those who maintained their heroic spirit in these times. "We need brotherhoods sealed in blood," he shouted, without paying attention to the one trying to quiet him, demanding executions and exemplary punishments. He asked for a chance to take part in the next job, making a show of firing a pistol with his two hands. He wanted to bring the man on the run toward the crude lights of a restaurant full of people. "Bring me something to eat," implored the other, remaining in the shadow of a pine tree. (There was still plenty of time before twelve; he wanted to show Someone who would be looking at His watch that he wasn't breaking the rule imposed on those who moan to approach the Bloodless Sacrifice.) Forgetting his request, the Scholarship Student returned with a bottle of liquor. The two of them walked toward the end of the avenue, where the sea broke in mute onslaughts on a fringe of reefs . . . Now they were sitting next to each other in the old public-bathing area, with its rectangular pools carved out of the rock, where the waves that flowed through a narrow, sea-urchin-covered passage died. The large wood house, whose roof sagged because its support beams were missing, creaked in every one of its loose boards whenever a gust of wind came along. A phosphorescence suddenly appeared in the larger pool, like a load of green floating wash that illuminated a worm-eaten bottom, pockmarked, where, among limpets whose shells looked like caterpillars, moray eels lying in wait poked out their heads. The floating exhalation went dim, and everything fell into darkness. "We should go back to human sacrifice," the Scholarship Student rattled on, "to the teocalli, where the priest squeezes out the fresh, juicy heart before tossing it onto a rotting pile of hearts; we should go back to the sacred horror of ritual immolations, to the flint knife that penetrates the flesh and slices open the rib cage . . ." The man on the run had heard the Scholarship Student's rhetoric ever since the days when both had studied in the same provincial school and talked over their plans for the future. "We belong to this world," he rambled on, his tongue growing thicker and thicker, "and we must return to our earliest traditions. We need chiefs and sacrificial priests, eagle warriors and leopard warriors; people like you." Several flashes of lightning suddenly lit up the pine shed, stained with green, falling apart, termite-eaten, where the two of them were lying at the edge of pools that stank of dried-out algae, of mollusks that had died in the sun, of the sea made foul by the city's garbage. "I'm hungry," moaned the man on the run, lying facedown. "Blessed is he that hungers," said the Scholarship Student, "in this city of gorged pigs, of those who hug their bellies." And now it was the song of praise for those who purified themselves by means of privation, the trials they endured, those who raised themselves to the level of knighthood. The other's fatigue was so great that he listened to the drunk speak without trying to follow his meanderings, enjoying the only satisfaction he still had in this misery:

108

that of feeling near him the presence of a voice that was not a danger signal. The Scholarship Student offered him the bottle. But the idea of swallowing that fiery liquid devoid of all consistency, all density, which lacked anything hard he could chew and feel pass down his throat, made him so nauseous that he pretended to fill his mouth by snapping his tongue and covering the mouth of the bottle with the palm of his hand so the smell wouldn't make him vomit. "The superman," the other went on, "the superman . . . the will to power"; his ideas were so fogged that he couldn't even follow his own exposition of an obscure theory that trailed off into shreds of sentences, interrupted by angry grunts and confused insults aimed at unnamed people. The man on the run decided to let himself fall asleep: the Scholarship Student, once he'd finished the bottle, would end up falling asleep as well or walking off without remembering where he'd been or with whom. He loosened his belt and his shirt collar, put his pistol—which weighed him down so much—on the ground, and let himself lie back with his eyes closed while his ears wandered from the words of the other, like a child drowsy from a lullaby whose words fade and disappear . . . Just as he was sinking into a nervous sleep, the other seized him by the arm, straightening him up with a shock. Near them, a man and a woman were tangled into a single silhouette. The higher head bent over the lower in an enveloping eagerness of arms that wrapped around each other. A lightning flash made it seem that both were black. Her dress began to float away, falling with its sleeves outstretched in a cloud of vetiver. The man grasped her around the waist,

109

bending her backward over a bench, and another lightning flash illuminated, just for a second, a body in metamorphosis, the beast with two backs moved by hushed moans that seemed more like the accompaniment to a cruel rite than a delightful embrace. Suddenly that knotted flesh slipped off the bench, like a wine cask falling over, without dividing or separating. "They are our strength!" exclaimed the Scholarship Student. "They are our strength!" The shadows stood up. The man walked aggressively toward the one who had shouted, while the woman huddled in a corner calling for her dress. The man on the run slipped away to the street while the noise of punches landing on soft flesh made him think the Scholarship Student was receiving blows he wasn't returning. Suddenly a long peal of thunder rumbled and the rain came. A warm, compact, swift rain, the kind that sweeps down from above, leaving the ground covered with dusty clots. Caught by the storm, the fugitive began to run toward the house with the Belvedere. But now the rain was pouring so heavily off the eaves, overflowing the gutters, pouring in streams onto the sidewalks, that he hurried to enter a café near the Concert Hall, impelled by an instinctive scruple to retain what decency remained to his dark suit. On seeing him, two men stood up. The man on the run understood, by the intensity in their eyes, by the way they slowly stood up, by the way each shifted a hand to his breast pocket, that they were going to execute him. His own hand sought out his pistol, clenching over its absence: the weapon had remained there, on the public beach. An ambulance was coming closer at full speed, its sirens screaming: the condemned man

110

threw himself in front of it, frightened out of his wits, running toward the lobby of the Concert Hall. The ambulance slammed on its brakes and stopped between his body and the hands frozen over their breast pockets.

(. . . and the musicians, their instruments looking like huge springs, finished playing the music for hunting dogs that have been blessed, finished the hunters' Mass; then came the silence he'd *heard* so often in the terrible solitude of the Belvedere—when the silhouette of a telephone lineman who had climbed up to the forest of green insulators that stood at the same height as the terrace took on the powers of the Angel of Death; after a pause comes the other music, the music in little jumps, with something to it of those toys very small children play with, the ones in which two parallel sticks are moved up and down so that two dolls take turns pounding a peg with mallets; now the broken waltzes would come, the trill of the flutes, and then the trumpets, the long trumpets, like those

115

played by the gilt angels on the cathedral organ where I made my First Communion; minutes, minutes left; then everyone would applaud and the lights would come on, all the lights; and it would be necessary to leave by one of the five doors; three behind me, which would be like one; two toward the park, which would be like one; they, the two of them, would be waiting outside, smoking, with their hands ready. Leave surrounded by people; put bodies around my body. But those two bodies will pass right through and swiftly scatter his cover; the woman with the fox stole will disappear; the man next to her will cross the park alone, useless for being alone; the man in front, whose neck I do not want to see, and the one on the left with his huffing and puffing, and the tall man with the nervous knees, and the young couple who listened with their brows furrowed, holding hands; and I will be left alone on the infinite length of the sidewalk made of soaked, slippery granite, so difficult to run on; I'll be alone, unprotected, unarmed, right in front of those men who will have all the time they need to raise their hands to their breast pockets, to aim, to squeeze the trigger without having to hurry, to empty a whole clip in a single volley. Oh! the howl, the eyes of that man who rode along ahead, that time, whose neck was scarred with acne—a neck so similar to this neck that I would have to find here, closer than that other when I caught it in the sights of my sawed-off shotgun . . . Those outside, those waiting for me were also looking toward the acne-scarred neck—don't look at it, don't look at it. "Take off the safety," said the tall one, who never forgot what had to be done in those situations and who later directed their escape. "Stay to the right,

116

always to the right, pass the truck, take a left, now the tunnel, careful," without ever meeting an obstacle, a police station or the lowered gates of a railroad crossing; the tall one who is out there, waiting for everyone to applaud and for the lights to go on, his eyes glued to the three doors which are like one or on the two doors which are like one, from the corner, where it's possible to see the five doors all at once. "Take off the safety," he'd say when the applause broke out and the lights went on and the porters opened the red curtains, making the rings click on the rods like poker chips . . . The box seats, all red in the half-light, the red plush of the chairs; the scarlet velvet of the railings; the wine color of the carpeting; a box like a house, like a bedroom, like a bed with high sides; go to sleep on the floor, on top of the smell of dust, my cheek among the tacks in the corner, my head sunken in the darkness, legs under chairs, as if under a roof, as if under roof tiles, red like the roof tiles of the tailor shop; lie down like a dog, on what's soft, what's bundled up, in whatever makes the floor softer; go back to the shacks of my childhood, made of boards, of debris, of cardboard, where I crouched down on rainy days along with the wet hens, when everything was moisture, bubbles, drainpipes—as it is now—and I didn't answer when people called me, because not answering when people called me made me enjoy being alone in the half-light even more, knowing I was being looked for in places where I wasn't . . . We've already reached the broken waltzes, which never quite become waltzes, the trill of the flutes; soon the trumpets, the long trumpets; and the woman with the fox stole is already picking up her stole and loosening something under her skirt that's bothering her, assuming all eyes are turned toward the orchestra; and throughout the entire audience, behaving as it would in church, there is an almost imperceptible flutter of hands, of sleeves, of fingers returned to bodies, the straightening, the gathering up of things exactly like what happens in church during the *Ite misa est*. I breathe deeply, calm, quite calm; I finally figured out what was so easy, so easy, much easier: the only easy thing. I won't leave. They'll applaud and the lights will go on, and then there will be confusion under the lights. They'll gather up their things, they'll slip on their furs; they'll take care to show off their jewels, they'll wave goodbye across the rows, saying that it was all magnificent, and they'll form groups, slow lines, toward the exits; and it will be easy to hide behind the curtains of one of the boxes, and wait until all of them have gone; wait until the doormen close the doors of the boxes, after they check to see if anything's been forgotten on the seats. And the two of them will think I've gone out with the audience, mixed in with them, surrounded; they'll think that they've lost my face among all those faces, that my body has blended in with too many other bodies together for them to see it; and they'll look for me outside, in the café, under the pergolas, behind the trees, behind the columns on the street where the saddlery is, on the street where the visiting-card printing shop is; they'll think, perhaps, that I've gone up to the old lady's apartment to hide out among the blacks at the wake; they might even go up themselves, and they'll see the body, shrunken in its box made of the poorest quality boards; they might even look for me

118

in the Belvedere, without suspecting that my pure things, my boxes of compasses, my first drawings are there inside the trunk. They won't think I stayed here. Nobody stays in a theater after the show is over. Nobody stays sitting in front of an empty, dark stage where nothing is being shown. They will close up the five exits with bolts and padlocks, and I'll stretch out on the red rug of that box over there—where the two in back have already gotten up—curled up like a dog. I'll sleep until dawn, until after it clears up at ten, until after midday. Sleep: the first thing is sleep. After that, a new era will begin.)

After that prodigious Scherzo, with its whirlwinds and its weapons, comes the Finale, a song of jubilation and freedom, with its celebrations and dances, its exultant marches and its laughter, and the rich volutes of its variations. And behold, amidst it all, Death, which lies beyond Victory, reappears. But once again Victory rejects Death. And the voice of Death is drowned out by the clamor of jubilation . . . The strings and woodwinds of the Presto were descending now in fortissimo toward the happy concerto for brass. "Can I open up yet?" asked the usher, seeing that the ticket seller was closing a book with a gesture of irritation, no longer paying any attention to what was being played behind the frayed damask curtain. Everything was exasperating him tonight: the symphony he had missed; the smell of the rain on his only suit; the forms of the flesh he had touched which still warmed his hands; the desire present in his throbbing heart, his annoyance at not being able to satisfy it; the penury of his obscure life—"in a cage"—and his messy room to make his insomnia all the more disagreeable. He berated Estrella in hushed tones, calling her what she was. And he recalled her complaints about the Inquisition and the things she'd said because she was threatened; she must have informed on someone; someone who'd relied on her, forgetting that a harlot is always a harlot, and her last name is garbage; it had to be that, because she'd informed on someone, she was trying to find excuses by working herself up: "that she might be thrown into the women's prison, that she might have to leave the neighborhood; that now they even wanted to know who you made a life with." And he'd listened to her without understanding, deaf to everything unrelated to the urgency of his desire. He slammed his fist down on the money drawer, but there was no satisfaction in it, repeating again and again the insult he preferred ever since he'd been thrown out of the house for want of a few coins. On his left, next to *Beethoven: His Great Creative Years*, printed on an official notice decorated with cut sugarcane, were the National Theater Regulations: *The employee in charge of the public sale of seats will take charge of the sealed currency in order to check it for any discrepancies, then turn over the money from his shift; in order to do so, he will close the ticket office half an hour before the end of the performance.* It was raining again, and the sound of the water on the nearby trees, on the sidewalk, on the granite of the stairs mixed in with the noise of the

121

applause that rose up in the theater. "Open up," said the ticket seller, locking his door. "The conductor is vile; the way he led the symphony, it couldn't have lasted its full forty-six minutes." He looked toward the old lady's terrace; soon he would go to make sure she was not the one who had died. The audience was rushing out of the hall, afraid the storm would get worse, with those winds blowing in from the sea, presaging the bad weather that had just been forecast by the weather bureau. The side doors were closed and only a few indecisive people stayed on among the mirrors and allegories in the lobby to discuss the performance.

Then, two spectators who had remained in their seats in the next-to-last row slowly stood up, crossed the deserted hall, whose lights were going out, leaned over the rail of a darkened box, and fired into the carpet. Some musicians came out onto the stage with their hats on, clutching their instruments, thinking that the shots might have been a strange effect of the storm, because just at that moment a prolonged crash of thunder echoed through the roof of the theater. "One less," said the policeman who had just been summoned, kicking at the body. "And besides, he was passing counterfeit money," said the ticket seller, showing the bill with the General with the sleepy eyes. "Give it to me," said the officer, seeing that it was perfectly good. "It will have to be included with the evidence in the case."

ALEJO CARPENTIER (1904–1980), Cuban novelist, essayist, and musicologist, is the author of *Explosion in a Cathedral, The Lost Steps,* and *Music in Cuba*, all available from the University of Minnesota Press.

ALFRED MACADAM is professor of Spanish and Latin American cultures at Columbia University. He has also translated works by Juan Carlos Onetti and Carlos Fuentes.

TIMOTHY BRENNAN is professor of cultural studies and comparative literature at the University of Minnesota. He is the author of *At Home in the World: Cosmopolitan Now* and *Salman Rushdie and the Third World: Myths of the Nation*.